UNINTENDED

A SIN SERIES STANDALONE NOVEL

GEORGIA CATES

GEORGIA CATES BOOKS, LLC

Published by Georgia Cates Books, LLC

Sign-up for Georgia's newsletter at www.georgiacates.com. Get the latest news, first look at teasers, and giveaways just for subscribers.

Editing services provided by Lisa Aurello

Formatting by Jeff Senter of Indie Formatting Services

Cover artwork by Jeff Senter of Indie Formatting Services

Cover photography by Lauren Perry of Perrywinkle Photography

ISBN-13: 978-1978304413 (CreateSpace-Assigned)

ISBN-10: 1978304412

KIERAN HENDRY

THIS DAY.

It's been a jack-in-the-box ever since I became a man. Dormant, but hiding inside its refuge, always threatening to make an appearance at any time. Each day has represented a crank of the handle controlling its release.

Today, it escaped.

It's time for me to fulfill my obligation to my new brotherhood. It's the burden that comes with being in a leadership role.

I must take a wife.

A wife I don't know. A wife born into a position at the top of a hierarchy. A wife who will forge a strong alliance between The Order and The Fellowship.

A wife I don't want.

I am Kieran Hendry. Eldest son of Lennox Hendry and Arabella Grieves Hendry, the new leaders of The Order. Many would kill to be in their position. Literally. But that isn't how the brotherhood works. We are born into the role. Like royalty.

My mother has been called home to preside over the brotherhood that her father and brother once led. My dad will act on her behalf until I'm ready to take my place as the leader of these people. My first act as their future leader will be to enter into a marriage treaty with a Fellowship woman. Bring peace between The Order and their enemy, The Fellowship.

I've been conditioned to accept an arranged marriage as my fate for as long as I can remember. Doesn't make it any easier though.

I always thought I'd marry from within The Syndicate, the brotherhood in which I was raised. I expected to forge a union with a woman I'd known my entire life, whose position within my brotherhood would strengthen my claim to leadership in the event of my paternal uncle's and cousins' deaths. A woman with virtue and purity who'd saved herself for her husband. Who the hell knows what I'll be getting with a woman from The Fellowship?

The Fellowship killed my maternal uncle and the brothers want retribution. They demand blood. A lot of it. But vengeance isn't our way. Revenge and death only yield rotting corpses. That isn't profitable: a dead man can't make money for us. Alliances. Those yield gain. Profit is always our focus.

My father pours two whiskies and brings one to me. "I know you need this; I still haven't forgotten what it felt like to hear my father tell me that I was going to marry a woman from The Order as part of a marriage treaty alliance."

I need more than one whisky. "I don't want a wife."

"I don't have to tell you that what you want doesn't matter. You're a Grieves and a Hendry. Future leader of The Order. Being at the helm of this organization means you don't get a choice. It's your duty to strengthen your brotherhood with an advantageous marriage. You will marry a woman from The Fellowship."

This marriage isn't something I can refuse. "Do I at least get to choose which woman I'll marry?"

"You have three choices." Well, at least there's that. "The most desirable is Abram Breckenridge's older daughter, Evanna. The next would be his younger daughter, Westlyn. Last choice is Sinclair's sister-in-law. Not a Breckenridge, or even a member of The Fellowship yet, but she will be soon."

"Why is the sister-in-law a consideration?"

"She's the sister of Bleu Breckenridge. Sinclair will do whatever it takes to maintain Ellison's safety because he wants to keep his wife happy."

An American who wasn't raised in a brotherhood. "She'll be weak."

"Agreed. Hence the reason she's your third choice. You'll only marry her if the other choices don't work out."

I've heard of Abram Breckenridge. None of it good. "What do you know about Abram's daughters?"

"Not a lot yet, but I've placed both under surveillance. We'll learn as much as we can before you choose."

It won't matter that The Order is under new leadership. "The Fellowship isn't going to willingly agree to an alliance with us, and Thane Breckenridge isn't going to hand over one of his nieces as a treaty bride."

"That's why we're going to force his hand by *taking* the bride of your choosing. He'll have no choice but to consider our proposition." My father pauses a moment. "And as a symbol of our good intention, I'm going to offer Shaw in marriage to his younger son or nephew."

Shaw is only eighteen. Still a child. And so headstrong. She has dreams and plans and ideas about the way she wants her life to go. My sister won't take well to being told she must marry anyone, treaty for the well-being of the brotherhood or not. "Won't my marriage suffice so Shaw doesn't have to marry?"

"Not with The Fellowship. There's too much bad blood between them and The Order. We have to propose an equal offering, or they'll never consider it."

"When is this going to happen?"

"As soon as you decide which woman you want."

I don't want any of them.

"I'll have a full report from the surveillance by the end of the week."

"Then I guess I'm claiming a wife this weekend." Which means I'm getting laid. I'm not pissed off about that.

"You'll need to bind your union to her as soon as possible." *Bind my union.* He means impregnate her. "Once your bairn is inside her, the claiming can't be undone by anyone."

A bairn. I don't want that either.

I was born nine months after my parents married. My father didn't waste any time *binding* his union with my mother. We've never discussed it, but I'm guessing he was persuaded to do so by his father just as he's doing with me now. "How did you feel when Grandfather told you that you were going to marry Mother?"

"I wasn't happy, but I knew taking Arabella as my wife was my duty to the brotherhood. Your mother and I both understood, and we made the most out of it."

Maybe theirs hasn't been a fairy tale romance, but my parents love and respect each other. And they share a common goal: they want the best for The Syndicate and The Order. That includes making this alliance with The Fellowship.

I'm the future leader of The Order. It's my job to ensure the prosperity of my brotherhood and those we're in alliance with. If that means taking a Fellowship woman as a wife and putting my child inside her then that's what I'll do.

Even if it's the last thing on earth that I want.

I'M a marksman for my brotherhood. An assassin. A hit man. But tonight I'm not ending the life of a loose end or an enemy or an opposition. The man I've been for the last twenty-eight years is the one being ended; I'll soon be mated to a Fellowship woman. Probably tonight.

"What can you tell me about the Fellowship women we're considering?"

My father sighs. "Bleu Breckenridge's sister is living with Thane's nephew. They're sharing a bedroom."

Good thing that one isn't a front-runner.

"And the older Breckenridge sister..." Dad pauses. "She's spending a lot of time with a Fellowship man. Behind closed doors. And overnight."

"What you're telling me is that two of my three choices are fucking other men?"

"Aye."

That eliminates both of them in my book. I won't have my wife hopping out of one man's bed and into mine.

"What of the younger Breckenridge sister?"

"My men saw nothing unbecoming."

"She hasn't kept the company of any man?"

"Westlyn's only interactions have been with family and female friends."

I could ask my father to tell me more about this woman, but the truth is that nothing he tells me will matter. She's the only option I'll consider for my wife at this point. "Where is she now?"

"I've been informed that she left her apartment with Sin's sister-in-law, and they just arrived at Duncan's Pub."

I have planned and carried out countless assassinations without so much as a qualm. But this… this, I dread like hell. I don't tolerate the weaker sex well. The tears. The whimpering. The whole fragility thing. I despise all of it.

But the pussy… I deal with that just fine.

"I've called Niall to bring the limo around."

What is my father thinking? "The limo will call too much attention."

"The limo will have the room you'll need for the men going with you."

I've never taken anyone with me on a job. "You know I work alone."

"This is different. You aren't shooting someone while you're perched at a distance. You're going into Fellowship territory, a place where they're always on guard, and you're going to take a woman of great value. No one person should attempt to do that."

I don't know the brothers of The Order yet. I don't trust them to carry this mission out flawlessly, but my father is right. I can't pull off this kidnapping by myself. "All right. I'll take four men from your surveillance team. But they need to understand that I expect them to stay the fuck out of my way. And fuckups won't be tolerated." If this effort fails, we'll likely not get another opportunity; Westlyn will be placed under a watchful eye. And that means I'll be forced to take one of the others as my bride.

I can't let that happen.

I'm surrounded by four men who've watched my wife-to-be for a week. They know more about her than I do, including what she looks like. I'm tempted to ask about her appearance, but I don't; these men have possibly seen parts of Westlyn Breckenridge that should be reserved for my eyes only. If I found out one of them had looked upon her unclothed, I'd be tempted to yank his eyeballs out of their sockets.

I've only had a few days to adjust to the idea of taking Westlyn as my mate. Don't ask me to explain it, but I already consider her my property although I've never laid eyes on her. My possessive feelings are completely insane, considering how much I don't want her or this marriage.

"Westlyn and Ellison… that's them coming out of the pub, boss."

They didn't stay long. I slide upward in my seat and watch the two women leaving the pub with a man. "Who is he?"

"Jamie Breckenridge."

Family. *Good girl, Westlyn.* "Drive slowly until we reach them. When the car stops, we'll exit together. First man who gets to Westlyn will hood her face and pull her into the backseat. Once she's inside, we're out of here."

"Jamie will be armed."

I'd expect no less. "I'll take care of him." I won't hesitate to put a bullet in him if he comes between me and my taking Westlyn tonight.

The back door opens, and we spill out of the car. Jamie Breckenridge moves in front of the two women, shoving both behind him. One of the women goes down, landing on the sidewalk.

He pulls his weapon just as I knew he would, but he doesn't stand a chance at this showdown. Gunman versus doctor. It isn't a fair fight.

My bullet enters his upper shoulder, the exact target I was aiming for. It isn't my intention to kill the man who is about to become my brother-in-law. Just need to hinder him a little.

He collapses to the sidewalk. One of the women screams and crawls to him on her hands and knees as though it's the end of the world. With that kind of reaction, I'm assuming that she's his American lover who wasn't raised in a brotherhood. A woman accustomed to these things wouldn't behave that way.

She places her hands over the growing wet sphere, leaning over him and saying things that I'm unable to hear.

"Get them in the car now."

Them? Here we go with the fuckups. This is why I work alone. I'm the only person I can depend on to get things right.

The other woman screams for help and fights impressively while Marshall holds her, and Glen places a hood over her head… before I'm able to see what she looks like. "Not both women. Just Westlyn Breckenridge."

"That's not what your father ordered."

He didn't mention anything about taking both women. "No time to argue. We need to go now." We likely only have seconds before The Fellowship brothers inside the pub realize that something has taken place.

The backseat of the limo fills, this time with two extra passengers. One more than I intended.

I'm not certain which of these women is my intended. I thought Marshall and Glen had Westlyn, but now I don't know since my father ordered both women to be taken.

"On your knees. Hands behind your back." I'm not worried about the MacAllister woman, but I'd expect Westlyn to have had extensive training on what to do in the event of an abduction. Can't be careless with that one.

A text comes in on the phone Glen has taken from one of their purses.

Fellowship: Let's talk.
Kieran: I'll consider that after I've had my fun.
Fellowship: Don't fucking touch them.

I'm amused by whomever is texting. Does this person really think he can tell me what to do?

Kieran: A little late for that. Don't come for them or they die.
Kieran: We'll contact you when we're ready to talk.

I toss the phone to Glen and he returns it to the purse. No need to ditch it. The Fellowship will trace us to the compound eventually anyway.

"Wes?" the woman to my right says. Her voice trembles, as does her body. She's like a frightened rabbit.

"I'm here." Westlyn Breckinridge hesitated before answering—and identifying herself. She's probably silently pleading with her friend to keep her mouth shut.

I flick my wrist at Glen, cueing him to skip binding Westlyn Breckinridge's wrists. I want her hands free.

"She's not Fellowship. You gain nothing by taking her."

I laugh at Miss Breckenridge's weak argument. "You don't think the sister of Sinclair's wife is powerful leverage? Sounds to me like Miss Breckenridge doesn't think very highly of you, Miss MacAllister."

Westlyn needs to learn sooner rather than later who it is she's dealing with. "Crawl to me, Westlyn. On all fours like the Fellowship bitch you are."

She pleases me when she does as she's instructed, proving she's able to follow orders. A good quality to have in a wife. "On your knees in front of me. Kneel before your master."

I'm going to be her leader. Her master. Her husband. She might as well get used to being on her knees in front of me. I plan on having her in that position often.

"Good lass. I think I'll reward you for following orders by taking off your hood." I lean forward and slowly lift the covering from her head.

I'm about to look into the eyes of the woman I'll call wife for the rest of my life. I'd be lying to myself if I said I wasn't mildly panicked about what I'm going to see.

The interior lights are on, and I stop lifting the cover to study the lower half of her face. No mustache. No beard. A narrow nose, slightly turned up on the end. A perfectly pouty set of pink lips with a deep cupid's bow.

I like what I see so far.

I remove the cover from her head, and her eyes blink several times before focusing on mine. Bold black strokes line the top of her eyelids with a slight wing on the outer corner. Long, lush lashes surround irises of… what color I can't tell. But they're much lighter than my nearly black ones.

Sexy. As. Fuck.

Niall accelerates and Westlyn tumbles toward me, breaking her fall with her hands on my upper thighs, her touch causing my dick to twitch. I'm instantly attracted to this woman, and it's a fucking relief like I've never known. "Hmm… no one told me you were such a beauty."

She stares at my face, and I imagine her mind rolling through images in her memory the way a thumb flips through pages of a magazine. "Should I know you?" Her voice and breathing are soft and steady, unlike her friend who's panting as though she might pass out at any moment.

"I'm Kieran Hendry."

A wrinkle forms and deepens across her forehead while her brows tense. "Are you part of The Order?"

"Aye. My mum is Arabella Grieves Hendry. Torrence was her brother."

The wrinkle across her brow lessens. "Your grandfather married your mum off to a brotherhood in the north as part of a treaty."

I'm pleased that she's familiar with my parents' marriage and treaty. "Aye. A very successful treaty, which made both brotherhoods very successful. And now The Order has asked her to come home and lead because she is the next Grieves blood successor."

That wrinkle in her forehead is back. "A woman is acting as the leader of The Order?"

"No. My father is acting on her behalf until I step into the role of leader." Not that my mother wouldn't make a powerful one. She's the strongest woman I've ever known, but she chose motherhood over leadership.

Niall quickly brakes and then accelerates again, forcing Westlyn to grip my thighs again when she loses her balance. "What are you going to do with us?"

"That conversation is coming, Miss Breckenridge, but right now I'm really enjoying the sight of you on your knees in front of me." I study her cupid's bow and consider reaching out to touch it. "I really like your pouty pink lips, but I think I'd like them more if they were wrapped around my cock."

She bears her pearly whites and snaps, "I hope you like my teeth as well."

That was unexpected. I'm impressed as hell with the bravery this woman is exhibiting. "Ouch, Miss Breckenridge. That could be dangerous for my dick. I guess we'll go with the original plan instead."

Her head tilts to the side and her expression is one I've seen on my little sister a thousand times. I call it her smart-ass face. "The original plan being...?"

"I take you to my house, tie you to my bed, and do whatever the fuck

I want to you." I look over at Miss MacAllister. "Both of you." Let's see what she has to say about that.

"Ellison isn't Fellowship."

"You said that already."

"She isn't one of us and doesn't understand any of this. She's simply the sister of a woman who married into the brotherhood. This isn't her fight. She doesn't deserve to be injured or... damaged."

I loved the way she substituted the word *damaged* for *raped*.

This may not be Ellison MacAllister's fight, but she will soon be part of The Fellowship. She isn't exempt from being used to my advantage. "Are you asking me to leave her unharmed?"

"Yes... please. Show her mercy."

Westlyn is protective of Ellison, but let's see how far that inclination runs. "What are you willing to do to keep Miss MacAllister safe?"

Westlyn hesitates a moment. "What do you want from me?"

I'm not ready to talk marriage just yet. I'm more interested in the fucking part now that I've seen her. "Will you take her beating? Take her rape? Plus yours?"

"No, Wes! Don't even think about agreeing to that."

The frightened rabbit has been very quiet until now, and I prefer that she stays silent. I flick my wrist, and Glen slaps Miss Macallister's face through the hood. "Shut. Your. Mouth. I'm negotiating with Miss Breckenridge."

"Ellison will be unharmed if I take hers and mine?" Our eyes lock, and her voice remains steady. This woman isn't afraid. Or at least doesn't appear to be.

Westlyn Breckenridge is willing to sacrifice herself for her friend. Selflessness. You don't come across many women with that quality. And I'm going to take advantage. "Yes, but one more stipulation, Miss Breckenridge. Take yours and hers without a fight. Submit to me freely, and I won't harm a hair on your friend's head."

"Swear it on the life of your firstborn son."

Those words are entertaining since she's going to be the one to give me my firstborn son. And she has no idea.

"Don't do this, Westlyn."

Westlyn acts as though she doesn't hear her friend's pleas. "Swear you'll not harm her. Swear it on the life of your firstborn son, Kieran Hendry, and I'll do it."

This will be a wonderful story to tell our son one day... how he was used to negotiate our first agreement before he was ever conceived.

"Miss Breckenridge of The Fellowship brotherhood, I swear to you on the life of my firstborn son that Miss MacAllister will not be harmed by me or any member of The Order." I can't resist dragging my knuckles down her baby-soft cheek. "Do we have a deal?"

She nods. "Deal."

The motion of the car soon stops, and Glen opens the door. "Take Miss MacAllister to the guest quarters. Feed her if she's hungry. Offer her a shower and change of clothes, but keep her confined there. You heard my deal with Miss Breckenridge. No harm is to come to her."

"Yes, sir."

I grasp Westlyn's wrist and lead her toward my suite. "Miss Breckenridge and I will be in my quarters. Do not disturb us under any circumstances." I have some claiming to do. And a firstborn son to conceive.

"Yes, sir."

"Wes... I... I'm so sorry," her friend calls out.

"It'll be okay, Elli. Go."

Westlyn doesn't know me. She has no idea what I'm capable of doing, and yet she's going to my quarters with me with her chin held high and her back straight as an arrow.

She's under the impression that she'll be raped and beaten enough for two women, but there are no tears. No whining. No pleading. I admire the strength she is displaying.

I open the door to my bedroom suite and hold out my hand. "Ladies first."

"I think you mean *captives* first." Damn, she has a smart-ass mouth on her for someone who was just kidnapped by her people's worst and most dangerous enemy.

"*Captive* works as well."

She enters and stands in the middle of the room, assessing her surroundings. "This is a very nice prison. My compliments to the decorator."

This woman is blowing my mind. How can she be brave enough to say such things? "Is this all part of some kind of training you've undergone?"

"I don't know what you mean."

Her reaction is flat. Emotionless. It's as though she's an empty body, and her mind isn't here with me. I don't like it, and I'm going to elicit some kind of reaction from her one way or another.

I pick her up and carry her to my bed, tossing her in the center. She lands on her back and presses her knees together. "You can close your legs all you like, but that isn't going to keep me from getting between them."

Her eyes widen as she watches me take off my jacket and go to work on the buttons of my shirt. It's the first hint of fear I've seen from her.

I leave my pants on and crawl up her body until we're face-to-face. "I thought you might want to finish undressing me."

No reply.

"What's wrong? You have nothing cheeky to say about that?" She turns her head, but I grasp her face and make her look at me. The grip of my hand on her cheeks forces her lips to protrude. "You make me want to fuck the sass right out of this pretty little mouth."

Still no reply. Disappointing. I was hoping for a little more of her smart mouth. I like it; it's something different since no one ever dares to provoke or challenge me.

I look into her eyes and study the flecks of color. Green. Brown. Gold. Such a lovely contrast next to her brown hair with golden streaks. I never dared to think, or hope, that my wife might be this beautiful.

Gorgeous women are always pursued, but gorgeous women with Westlyn's footing within The Fellowship would be highly sought. "How many cocks have been inside you?" There's a sharp hitch in her breath, as though I may have offended her. "Tell me now."

Her eyes narrow. "So many that I can't remember them all."

So many that I can't remember them all. That makes me see fucking red.

A Fellowship whore. That's who my wife will be. I should have known, but I had hoped that there was a chance that she had remained pure.

Wrong.

"If you've had so many that you can't remember them all, then one more won't bother you. I promise you that you'll not have a problem remembering this one." I push my hand up the bottom of her dress. "I'm going to fuck you as often as I want and as hard as I want, and you're not going to tell me I can't." I feel for the crotch of her knickers and yank it so hard that the fabric rips apart. "How many of those men have been inside you without protection?"

She stares at the ceiling, saying nothing, and blinks rapidly.

I lower my body, so there's only an inch or so between our faces. "Answer me now, Westlyn."

"Fuck. You."

Is she trying to piss me off? Make this worse than it has to be? "Oh, you're definitely about to do that, Fellowship whore."

Her eyes narrow. "You are a *monster*. You're going to be the perfect leader for The Order."

Her words penetrate my rage and seep into the rational corner of my mind, the part that tells me I'm allowing my anger to take over. If I don't get myself under control, I could truly hurt her.

I'm a leader. I can't allow emotions to dominate me. Ever.

This woman has the power to affect me. Affect my actions. My emotions. It's a weakness I can't afford.

I push away from her and sit back on my haunches, looking at her lying on the bed with her knees pressed together like an innocent virgin. "You shouldn't have defiled your body by being with all of those men." I move off her and go to the bench to grab my shirt. "You should have kept yourself pure for your husband."

Pure for me.

She says nothing, but pulls the bottom of her dress downward to cover her legs and scoots to the head of the bed.

I go into my closet and fetch the long white silk gown my mother chose for her *virginal* daughter-in-law. Not this woman who freely gives her body to men. Not this woman who has no honor.

I toss the gown on the bed at her feet. "Put on this gown while I'm gone and expect to finish this when I return."

CHAPTER TWO
WESTLYN BRECKENRIDGE

KIERAN HENDRY ASKED me how many dicks I'd had inside me, and I couldn't bring myself to give him the pleasure of knowing that his would be the first. My virginity isn't his for the taking. It should belong to my future husband, but thanks to him, that's never going to happen.

I'm not sure why he stopped. Maybe it's his cruel way of prolonging my dread and fear, but he seemed angry to hear that he wouldn't be my first. Why? Why would a brother from The Order care if I was a virgin or not?

I touch the fabric of the gown he tossed on the bed. So soft and silky. Exquisite. Expensive. Why does he have this beautiful gown? It looks like something a bride would wear on her wedding night. And why does he want me to wear it? What purpose does it serve?

I don't understand what's happening. I don't understand why he was angered when I told him I'd been with other men. And I don't understand why he'd be so offended by my virginity not being intact for my husband.

Why does he care?

I don't want to put on the gown, but I'm afraid not to. Kieran Hendry and I made an agreement, and he could harm Ellison if I don't do as he orders. I can't allow harm to come to my dear friend when I have the power to prevent it.

A tear slides down my cheek as I recall my brother lying on the ground, shot and bleeding. My pain and fear at being stuck in this compound are doubled because I have no idea if Jamie is dead or alive. And neither does Ellison. She must be losing her mind right now.

I love Jamie. He's one of the few people on this earth who understands me. I can't lose him. I can't.

I lie down on the bed and recall the things that Kieran said to me.

You make me want to fuck the sass right out of this pretty little mouth.

I'm going to fuck you as often as I want and as hard as I want, and you're not going to tell me I can't.

Expect to finish this when I return.

He's going to do horrid things to me when he comes back. And I agreed to let him without a fight.

This is how I'm going to lose my virginity. Raped by the new leader of The Order. Sullied in the eyes of the Fellowship brothers. Not one of them will have me as his wife after this.

Who am I kidding? Raped by The Order's leader or not, no Fellowship man was going to claim or marry me anyway. My father ensured that outcome. He made certain that every brother knew I was off-limits. Not one would give me the time of day. Good thing I never planned on being with a Fellowship brother because I'll never find one who'll have me when Kieran Hendry is finished with me.

My father is dead, and the brothers still won't so much as look in my direction. It's as though they're afraid Abram Breckenridge will rise from the grave and fulfill this threat to massacre any man who touches me. I almost wish the evil bastard were still alive so he could make this Kieran Hendry asshole sorry for everything he does to me.

I decided a while ago that I would never marry a Fellowship man, but I always believed it would be on my terms. Not because I'd been ruined by the new Order leader.

Life in Edinburgh with The Fellowship is the only life I've ever known. Where will I go after I'm considered tainted goods? What will I do with my life?

I jolt when there's a knock at the door. Who is knocking and asking permission to enter the room where a captive is being held? "Come in?"

The door opens and a short, stocky woman with solid gray hair pushes a table filled with food into the room. "Hello, dear. I'm Mrs. Bruce. Mr. Hendry asked me to bring your dinner while you wait for his return." She looks at the crumpled gown on the bed. "He also asked me to assist you in preparing for bed."

Dinner... I understand that, but rapists don't send little old ladies to prepare their victims for sexual assaults. "Did Kieran leave the compound?"

"Yes. He and the other Mr. Hendry had a meeting to attend."

A spark of hope ignites inside me. Perhaps they were contacted by Thane to negotiate for our return? He and Sin and Jamie won't leave Ellison and me with these people. I know they won't.

Mrs. Bruce uncovers the smallest of the three plates on the table. "Mr. Hendry wants you to have oysters."

"Why in the world would that man care anything about what I eat?"

"Oysters get the juices flowing."

"What juices?"

She lifts her brows and looks downward. "Those juices. The womanly ones that put you in the mood for loving."

What. The. Hell?

"Eat up, Miss Breckenridge. He'll expect you to be ready when he returns."

I'll be ready. Ready to leave.

"Please, Miss Breckenridge. I don't want Mr. Hendry to be angry with me because you aren't ready when he returns."

These aren't logical people. They might physically harm this old woman because I didn't eat these damn oysters. "All right." I lift the shell and swallow the first of the half-dozen oysters on the plate. Mmm... nice and briny. One of the best oysters I've ever had.

"You're a lucky girl. Mr. Hendry could have had his pick of girls, but he chose you. Not everyone is pleased about his decision, but I for one couldn't be happier. It's time this happened."

Someone has lied to this poor woman. "I don't think you understand why I'm here."

"I understand perfectly." She uncovers a plate of duck confit and risotto. "Eat up. You'll need your strength."

I eat what I force down, only because I don't want this woman harmed, and Mrs. Bruce covers the dishes when I finish. "You didn't eat much."

"Nervous stomach."

"No need to be nervous. Mr. Hendry is going to make you a very happy woman tonight."

Happy? I don't think so.

"Come with me. It's time for your shower."

Mrs. Bruce goes to the bed and fetches the gown, frowning when she holds it up for inspection. "He'll be back soon, so there's no time to iron it. I'll hang it on the back of the door, and we'll hope that the steam loosens the crinkles."

She goes into the bathroom and turns on the water but doesn't come out. "Time's wasting. Get in here, lass."

I go into the bathroom, and she still doesn't leave.

"Go on. Turn around."

I do as she says and she lowers the zipper of my dress. "I'll launder your clothes for you if you wish to keep them."

Of course, I want to keep my clothes. What else would I wear home? "I don't think you'll have time to launder them."

I slide the dress down my body, and it takes my ripped knickers to the floor with it. Mrs. Bruce bends down and lifts them from the floor. "Oh dear."

"He ripped them."

"I see that. Would you like me to throw them out?"

"Yes, please." I want no reminders of any interaction I have with Kieran Hendry.

I cover my breasts with one arm while using the other to hold out my bra.

"No need to be timid with me. It's my job to assist Hendry women as needed."

But I'm not a Hendry woman. "Do you know anything about my friend, Ellison?"

"I prepared a meal for her, but someone else delivered it to her room."

"Is she okay?"

"I have no reason to believe she isn't."

Mrs. Bruce flicks her hand toward the shower. "Get in, lass. Mr. Hendry will be back before we know it, and he'll be angry if you aren't ready."

Kieran Hendry is an even bigger monster than I thought for making this sweet old lady prepare me for the things he's going to do to me.

God, I hope there's a negotiation in the works for Ellison and me.

I stand beneath the hot water and imagine what it will feel like to have him on top of me, between my legs. He's well over six feet tall. Every bit of fifteen stones. He lifted and carried me over his shoulder in what felt like one smooth motion. He tossed me onto the bed as though I weighed nothing. No part of him that I'm able to see is small. I'm guessing that includes his cock as well.

I wonder if he'll be violent. "Have you done this before?"

"Done what, dear?"

"Prepared a woman for Kieran?"

She looks confused by my question. "Of course not; you're the first."

"Will you tend to me afterward?"

"No. That's for Kieran to do." She giggles. "You truly are an innocent lass, aren't you?"

"I've never been with a man." By force or voluntarily.

"Maybe I should ask Mrs. Hendry to come in and talk to you? She might be able to ease your nerves a bit."

Kieran's mother might listen to me. I could plead with her, woman to woman, to stop her son from violating me. "Yes. I would like to see her. Will you go get her now?" Before Kieran comes back.

"Let's finish with you first so that you're ready when Mr. Hendry returns, and then if there's time, I'll have her come in."

I quickly rinse the conditioner from my hair. "I'm done." I turn off the water and step around the glass door to where Mrs. Bruce is standing with an outstretched lush white robe for me. Reminds me of the way my nanny, Iona, would wrap me in a towel after my bath when I was a child.

I tie the belt around my waist and twist a towel around my wet hair. Mrs. Bruce removes the white gown from the hook on the back of the door and shakes it. "The steam helped. Good thing because I certainly wouldn't want Mrs. Hendry to see that I put you in a wrinkled mess." She returns the gown to the hook. "Let's comb your hair and dry it. Mr. Hendry won't like you coming to bed with wet hair."

I don't have time for this. I need to speak to Kieran's mother before he comes back. I snatch the comb from her hand and all but rip out my hair as I drag it through the tangles. I lean over and dry my hair on hot and high as I shake it out with my fingers. It's a wild, bushy mess when I stand upright. "Miss Breckenridge... I think we should smooth your hair."

"It's fine."

"Kieran won't like it... so big."

Fuck Kieran and what he likes. "Do you have a flat iron?"

"Miss Hendry does. I can get it."

"Please do. And bring her with you when you return."

"The Miss Hendry I was referring to is Shaw, Kieran's sister."

How many Hendrys are there? And will they all be in this house doing nothing while I'm being assaulted?

"We should probably hurry. Don't want to keep Kieran waiting because I'm not ready."

"Yes, Miss Breckenridge." She holds out a brush. "You should probably try to tame that while I'm gone."

Mrs. Bruce returns, and she straightens my bushy hair. She's slow as fuck. "I bet Mr. Hendry loves your long hair. He's never been fond of short on women."

Again, fuck Kieran and what he likes. "Can you go get Mrs. Hendry now?"

Mrs. Bruce smiles. "Yes, but let's get you into your gown first. Arms up."

She dresses me as though I'm a toddler and can't do it for myself. It would be completely annoying if I had time to be annoyed.

"It's endearing that you're so nervous."

Endearing? I'm about to be brutalized. What the fuck could be endearing about that? "Can you please hurry, Mrs. Bruce? I'm afraid Kieran will be here any minute."

"Of course."

This is my last hope. If Kieran's mother has no mercy on me, it's over. I'm his to do with as he pleases.

CHAPTER THREE

KIERAN HENDRY

THE FELLOWSHIP COUNCIL of Breckenridge men stands when we enter. It's a show of respect, but we aren't held in high regard by them. And they aren't pleased by our presence. "Welcome. I'm Thane Breckenridge. These are my sons, Sinclair and Mitch. And my nephew, Jamie Breckenridge—Abram's son."

"I'm Lennox Hendry. These are my sons, Kieran, Maddock, Calder, and Carson."

Thane nods. "Come. Sit. Let's have a drink."

A red-haired woman enters the dining room with a serving tray of glasses and a large bottle of dark amber. Since it's the place of the hosting leader's wife to serve when two councils meet, I assume this woman must be Thane's wife, Isobel.

"Every great meeting has always begun with a fine whisky. Don't you agree?" Thane says.

My father nods but his eyes are on the redhead. As if he knows her. "Aye. Indeed."

She serves us first and works her way around the table until everyone has a glass of whisky. I watch my father watching her. She never once looks him in the face, but I'm convinced this isn't their first meeting. A man doesn't look at a woman like that unless something has transpired between them.

"Anything else, Thane?" Isobel asks.

"That'll be all. Thank you."

The woman leaves, and Thane holds up his glass. "Here's to a productive meeting where we're able to come to a mutual agreement."

The warm liquid burns all the way down. I'd like a dozen more just like it to numb the anger I feel toward Westlyn for giving her body to countless men. For ruining what could have been something good between us in a situation neither of us can escape. But now I'm going to be stuck with a whore for a wife, and she's going to be stuck with a husband who despises her for what she's done.

It's customary for the two leaders to lead the conversation when two brotherhoods meet, and my father is the one to initiate the discussion. "You're aware of my backstory with Arabella? How she came to be my wife as part of a treaty?"

"Aye."

"At The Syndicate, our belief is to operate with as few rivals as possible. And The Order has far too many powerful adversaries to ever function at its full capacity. We'd like to change the way it operates to mimic The Syndicate. That means making you our allies rather than our enemies."

"The Order has been a cruel group of people. What makes you sure that as a whole, they're going to support this reversal?"

Thane isn't mistaken. The Order was a cruel group of individuals under my uncle's leadership, but that stops here. That kind of behavior is counterproductive and will not be tolerated under our leadership.

"The people of The Order enjoy brutality because Torrence did. It's what they were taught. It's all they know. They need to be retrained to enjoy something else. I can do that."

Thane doesn't look convinced. "How do you propose to accomplish such drastic change?"

"Only one way—rule over them with an iron fist that they fear. Sure, it'll take making examples out of some brothers, but I'm prepared to do it. A few public executions always put people in their place."

Executions aren't something we take pleasure in but they are often necessary.

"Our people will be resistant to this alliance," Thane says.

Resistance by The Fellowship isn't the least bit unexpected.

"I understand there's been a lot of spilled blood between the two, but the benefits of partnering with us outweigh any grudge you hold. It will do nothing but benefit you and your people once we get things on track."

Thane hesitates. "If we do it, I would have to insist on some type of insurance."

Jamie's eyes widen and his fist tightens, stretching the skin on top of his hand so taut that the blue veins appear as though they're trying to escape. If he isn't happy right now, he damn sure isn't going to be happy about what my father is going to say next.

"We're prepared to give you that, and we want our own insurance. We'd like to propose a double treaty. We take Westlyn or Evanna Breckenridge or Ellison MacAllister as a wife for Kieran, and as a sign of good faith, I'll give you my daughter, Shaw, to be married to Mitch or Jamie."

Jamie Breckenridge's face is blood red. I bet his blood pressure is nearly at stroke level. "We'll never give a one of them to you."

I chuckle, wondering if he has so quickly forgotten that we have his sister and lover. "You didn't give us Westlyn and Ellison, but we have both of them."

"You're not keeping Ellison or my sister."

Sinclair Breckenridge holds out his hand in Jamie's direction. I'm not part of their brotherhood, but I recognize the hand gesture as a warning to not overstep his boundaries. "Jamie, you sit on the council, but this isn't your choice. Dad and I will make the decision based upon what's in the best interest of our people as a whole."

"We need Kieran's wife to be a Breckenridge—or the equivalent—so we're on equal footing. I fully trust that this partnership will work, and it won't come down to an eye for an eye. I wouldn't be offering you my only daughter if I didn't believe it would be successful."

Thane looks at Sin and then back to my father. "We can't make this kind of decision tonight. We need time to discuss it."

I don't think we could make a snap decision about something this important either, but they need to understand that their women aren't coming home until a resolve is reached. "In the meantime, we're keeping Westlyn and Ellison."

"No. You can't agree to this, Thane."

There goes Jamie overstepping his boundaries again. Maybe it's time I set him straight on how this is going to play out.

"The part where we keep Westlyn and Ellison is nonnegotiable. I need time with them to help me decide which one I'll take as my wife. If I like neither, then I'll need a few days with Evanna."

"You'll take none of them as your wife."

Jamie Breckenridge doesn't know me or how I tick. I don't take well to being told what I will and won't do. Especially by a leader's nephew who will never be the head of his brotherhood.

I grin and lick my lips. "I plan on tasting one of them tonight. Maybe both. I haven't decided yet." Aye, I'm being a dick. Taunting a man who is probably about to lose his mind with fear for his sister and lover, but he has opened his mouth more than once when he shouldn't have. He needs to learn his place.

"That's enough, Kieran," my father warns.

"Don't you fucking touch either of them."

Despite being a doctor, the dumb bastard is a slow learner. "Who's going to stop me?"

"I will kill you."

He stands and pulls his Glock, aiming it directly at my face. Not the first time I've looked down a barrel. Hell, it's not even the second or third or fourth.

"That's not a good way to begin the treaty." Does the dumb bastard forget that we're here because we want peace and prosperity?

"You weren't thinking that when you put a bullet in me a few hours ago."

He seems a little pissed off about that. "You pulled your weapon. We had no choice."

"You were kidnapping two of our women. Of course, I was going to pull my weapon."

Okay. I can't say that I blame him for that. "It wasn't our intention to kill you. Otherwise, you'd be dead." Jamie Breckenridge doesn't know that I'm a sniper. He has no idea that I never miss my target. Ever. If I wanted that bullet to go into his heart, it would have.

"Stand down, Jamie." He doesn't move. "Now," Thane adds.

He does as Thane orders and sits, staring a hole through me as though he's the taunter. I don't think so. "I will have three days with them. Not a minute less. Who knows? Maybe one of them will be carrying my heir by the time they return, and the decision will be made for me."

He slams his fist on the table. "Nooo!"

"That's our offer. We'll contact you in three days. And just in case you're thinking of coming for them, we won't hesitate to put bullets in their pretty little heads. Enjoy the rest of your night."

The Syndicate isn't called the sleeping giant for no reason. We are a peaceful people until our hand is forced. After that, we're out for blood.

The limo is pulling away from Thane Breckenridge's property when the car slows. "There's a woman in the drive, Mr. Hendry."

"Stop the car."

My father opens the door to get out, but Isobel pushes her way inside the car. "Isobel. It's good to see you. I wanted to say something earlier but…"

"I know. It's good tae see ye too. I wish we had time tae visit, but I only have a few minutes before I'm missed."

I was right. My dad knows Thane's wife.

"What is it, Issy?"

"I need to speak tae yer son aboot my niece." She looks at me. "Westlyn is Abram and Torrie's daughter. There isn't a reason in the world that she should be anything other than a monster with those two for parents, but she isn't. Wes is kind… loyal… dutiful… *and pure*. My niece is beautiful inside and oot. She'll make a wonderful wife for ye, unless ye choose tae mishandle her while she's in yer care. In that case, she'll come tae despise ye, and believe me, existence is miserable when ye're shackled tae someone ye hate."

Pure. That word catches my attention. "Westlyn Breckenridge is *pure*?"

"Abram might have been a mean bastard, but he made sure that Westlyn wasn't touched by any brother. He was saving her for someone. It ultimately didn't work oot, and no man has reached oot tae Thane tae declare interest in her."

Abram was saving Westlyn for someone but not his older daughter? There must be a reason for that, but what? "Abram is dead. He's no longer here to ensure his daughter's purity."

"True, but Thane and Sin have taken responsibility for Wes. Tae taint her would be an offense against them. She remains a virgin. Of that, I'm certain."

Not according to Westlyn. "Why would she claim otherwise when I asked?"

"Wes is being the strong, resilient captive she was trained tae be. She sees ye as part of The Order that she loathes. There's no way she'd voluntarily tell ye that she's a virgin. Think aboot it. That's the one sure way tae get yerself violated by yer brotherhood's enemy."

"We've kidnapped two of your women. Why would you volunteer this information?"

"I know Lennox, and I believe in the marriage treaties he's proposing, but I do it also because I love Westlyn. I dinnae want her tae be mistreated because she's misunderstood or is doing as she's been taught."

"Thank you for coming to us, Issy."

Issy. That name rolls off my father's tongue in a very familiar manner.

"I appreciate the risk you took by coming out to speak to us."

"I love my niece. I would do anything for her."

I'm not sure what it is I see in my father's eyes as he watches Isobel Breckenridge get out of the car. I wish I knew what had happened between them. Or maybe I don't.

"Can we trust her?"

"Aye. I've known her since I was sixteen. She would never purposely mislead me. If she says Westlyn is pure then she believes it."

My father didn't get to the place he's in because he's unwise. "If you tell me I can trust her, then I will. No question."

I don't believe that Westlyn is the whore she claims to be. The more I think about her actions and words, the more I am convinced that Isobel Breckenridge is right. I recognize the survival tactics Westlyn was using to protect herself… from me. Because she sees me as the enemy.

And it changes everything.

CHAPTER FOUR
WESTLYN BRECKENRIDGE

COME ON. Come on. Come on, Mrs. Hendry. Get in here. Get in here now.

My heart is pounding in my chest, pulsating in my face, thumping in my ears. I've never experienced a direr time in my life. My life is literally in the hands of this monster's mother.

Maybe she hates this life as much as I do. Maybe she'll understand. Maybe she'll be merciful.

But fuck. His mother is the sister of Torrence Grieves. My family killed him. She's going to want to see me beaten and bloody if she's anything like her sadistic brother.

I'm on the verge of seeing oysters and duck confit again when the door opens. No knock. Just a tall, broad body filling the doorway.

It's over. The hope I had, although small, is gone.

Kieran closes the door and the clicking sound of the lock signifies the start of what is going to be a night of hell. My first inclination is to run, but to where I don't know. I suppose I could lock myself inside the bathroom, but that would only delay the inevitable for a few minutes. I'd probably only manage to piss him off and make it worse for myself.

He crosses the room to the small bar and pours two whiskies. "Come sit with me."

I'm motionless as I watch him move from the bar to the sofa.

"It's okay, Westlyn. I'm not going to hurt you. I promise."

I'm not convinced; I don't trust him.

"Come have a whisky with me, and let's talk."

I go to the sofa and sit beside him, my tailbone on the edge… just like my nerves. I down the entire glass of amber liquid, hoping it will numb whatever comes next.

"Want another?"

"Yes." I want the whole bottle.

Kieran takes my glass and refills it. "I mistreated you, and I'm sorry for that."

He's mocking me, and that pisses me off. Does he want me to play the weepy victim? Fuck that. "Bullshit. You enjoyed terrorizing me."

"I lost my temper and acted out of anger. I was wrong for that."

I look at him, speechless. I think a feather could knock me over at this point.

"It's not in my nature to apologize. Ever. I hope you'll see it for the rarity it is."

"Why are you apologizing to me?"

"Because I want a do-over."

"Which part? The one where you kidnap me and shoot my brother? Or the one where you tell me you're going to rape and beat me enough for two women? Or the one where you toss me on the bed and rip my knickers?" I should keep my mouth shut and not antagonize him, but I can't stop talking.

"I'm aware of my bad behavior, and I'd very much like a chance to show you a different side of me."

Monsters only have one side. "I don't know what kind of trick this is, but I'm not falling for it."

"I'm not trying to trick you or play games."

I'm not some stupid woman who will melt because this handsome man is saying all of the perfect things. "I don't believe you."

"I can see why you wouldn't." He takes a big drink of whisky. "I've just been to meet with The Fellowship council."

My thoughts instantly go to Jamie. "My brother was there?"

"Aye. He's alive and well. A sore shoulder, I'm sure, but he'll recover fully."

What a relief. Kieran spoke with the council. That must mean that Thane negotiated for our return, and he's here to take me home. I know he'd never leave me with these people. "May I have something else to wear?" There's a chance I won't be considered tainted if I'm returned only a few hours after being taken, but that won't be the case if I'm returned wearing this gown.

"You aren't going home."

I don't understand. "You said you met with the council."

"We did. So we could tell them our conditions for returning Ellison and you."

"What are your conditions?"

"There are going to be two marriage treaties to bring peace between The Fellowship and The Order. My sister, Shaw, is going to take a Fellowship husband, and I'm going to take a Fellowship wife. I have three choices: Evanna, Ellison, or you." His eyes lock on mine. "And I want you."

Marriage treaty? For peace? This is crazy. There's no way The Fellowship and The Order will ever live in peace. I'd just be sucked into a group of monsters. Monsters who'd probably kill me first chance they got. "I won't marry you."

"Believe me, I didn't want this either. I was mad as hell when my father told me that I was going to marry a Fellowship woman. But then I saw you and heard your smart mouth… and saw your strength and defiance and selflessness. I like it. And I know it's crazy as hell, but I've decided that I want this union." He places his glass of whisky on the cocktail table and slides closer, making me flinch. "I want you to be my wife."

This makes zero sense. "You don't know me. How can you say that you want me to be your wife?"

"Arranged marriages can go wrong very quickly. If the two people don't despise each other, that's considered a plus."

"But I do despise you."

"You despise the way I treated you. There's a difference. And that's why I want a do-over. I want to show you that I'm not the person you believe I am."

He's had about an hour to show me who he is. He's probably much worse than I think. "You didn't answer my question. How can you say that you want me to be your wife?"

"I have to marry one of you… and I think I may like you." He reaches out and drags his knuckles down my face. "You're beautiful… and I'm incredibly attracted to you. I don't think that's a bad start for an arranged marriage."

This guy is unbelievable. "You terrorized me. Made me fear for my safety."

"You bragged about being with countless men. It angered me to hear my wife-to-be boast about such things, and I lashed out."

"I'm not your *wife-to-be*."

"I want you to be."

If that angers him so badly, then why choose me? "You want me as your wife even though I've been fucked by half the brothers of The Fellowship?"

He chuckles. "You haven't been fucked by anyone. Isobel confirmed it."

I don't believe him. Isobel wouldn't confide in him. She wouldn't betray me. "Liar."

"I'm not lying."

"Prove it."

"Isobel and my father are old acquaintances, and she snuck away from Thane and the council to speak to us. She told me that you were nothing like your parents. Instead, you are kind. Loyal. Dutiful. *Pure*. Beautiful inside and out. Those are the words she used to describe you. She said you would make a wonderful wife unless I mishandled you while you were in my care. Her warning was clear: you'd hate me if I mistreated you, and we'd both be miserable if we married under those conditions."

"That proves nothing."

"Your father ensured that you were to never be touched by a brother; you were being saved for someone, but it didn't work out. Now that your father is dead, Thane and Sin have taken responsibility for you. To dishonor you would be an offense against them. And no brother would dare offend his leaders."

I don't have an argument. He's right, and we both know it.

"You lied about being with those men to protect yourself. Because you understand the pricelessness of remaining a virgin in a world like ours. It makes and breaks women all the time."

And it's so unfair. The brothers can fuck around whenever they feel like it, and yet we must remain *pure* for them. It's another one of the things I hate about this life.

"Your aunt believes in what we're proposing because the treaties will bring peace. And she supports your marriage to me."

"Nothing that you just said proves anything."

"Perhaps not, but I will marry one of you. Are you really going to make me take Ellison from your brother? Or will you stand by and watch Evanna lose Craig, the one and only man she has ever loved, while no brother awaits your return?"

"That's a cruel thing to say." And correct.

"Cruelty isn't my intention. I say it to remind you that there isn't a Fellowship man who wants you, but that doesn't mean that *no* man wants you." He moves off the couch to the floor onto one knee. He takes a ring from the interior pocket of his jacket. "Be my wife."

I've dreamt of a man who would kneel before me with a diamond ring and pretty words. A man who adored me. Not one who narrowed me down from a choice of three. I don't want to be a man's wife because he settled.

But it's not like there's a better offer on the table. No Fellowship man wants me. And no Fellowship man will have me after I stay here three days. Doesn't matter if Kieran touches me or not because the worst will be assumed. The longer I'm here, the more brothers will presume. I know what happens to the women who return to The Fellowship after they've been taken by The Order. They never marry. They live as outcasts or end their lives.

Outcast among The Fellowship? Or wife of The Order's leader and mother of the future leaders of the brotherhood? Those are my two options.

The choice is a simple one because there is no good alternative, but I can't make that kind of commitment at this point. If I tell him yes now, he'll want to claim me. There will be no going back after that.

"I'll consider marrying you." He grins, looking so sure that he's getting what he wants, and it pisses me off. "I said I'd think about it. That's not a yes." Kieran Hendry has been a bastard to me tonight. He owes me restitution.

He slides an enormous diamond ring on my finger, and it's a perfect fit. He lifts my hand and studies the ring on my finger. "It looks good on you."

I don't even know how many carats it could be, but it's a lot bigger than my mum's. And hers isn't small.

"This was my grandmother's wedding ring. A wee bit more than seven carats. Exceptional color and clarity. My grandfather paid more than fifty thousand pounds for it fifty years ago. Don't lose it."

The ring is gorgeous, but it doesn't make me lose my good sense. "Did you not listen to what I just said? Consideration isn't an affirmative."

"You're going to say yes, and we both know it."

Such a confident arse. He's used to getting everything he wants, but he isn't going to snap his fingers and make me jump. "No, we don't both know it. It's going to take work on your part to convince me after the way you've treated me tonight."

"I've never worked to win a woman in my life."

I don't doubt that being the truth for a second. I bet he could charm the pants off any woman. Except me.

"There's a first time for everything."

"Do you know how many women from The Order and The Syndicate would jump at the opportunity to be my wife?"

I'd guess most of them. "I don't know, and I don't give a damn."

"They'd line up for the chance to be in my bed for just one night."

Kieran is a leader. That alone makes him a desirable mate, but he's also handsome. Black hair. Nearly black eyes. Tall and broad and muscular. I saw the bulging muscles in his chest and arms when he took off his shirt earlier. I'm certain that he's highly sought after by the women of The Order and The Syndicate.

"That would end if I were your wife. I won't allow you to infect me with your whores' sexual diseases."

"I would never put the health of my children's mother at risk."

I guess that's sort of a sweet thing to say, but I don't buy it. "That's a bold statement to make when you've never had to be faithful to one woman." I'm not stupid. I know leaders aren't monogamous. They fuck whoever, whenever they like. Except Sin: he's the exception to the rule. I'm certain that he'd never cheat on Bleu. He loves her and the babies too much to ever so much as consider betraying them.

"I'll be a good and faithful mate because it's what you ask of me. As your husband, I would want to please you."

I'm surprised to hear him say that. Men in leadership roles are usually only concerned with their own pleasure. "You want to please me?"

"I very much want to please you. And I plan on doing so as soon as you'll let me."

"So now you want my permission instead of my submission?"

"I'd take you any way you'd give yourself to me."

Evanna and Bleu and Ellison talk about their sex lives all the time. I pretend I've had experiences as well, but the truth is that I've never even made out with a guy. One stolen kiss when I was sixteen. That's it.

I'm not a dope. I know how things happen, but it isn't the same for all couples. The different stories I hear from my friends are evidence of that.

Evanna loves Craig. Bleu loves Sin. Ellison loves Jamie. I don't love Kieran. Shite, I don't even like him. He's a total dick. But a good-looking dick. And his body is very hot. I'm curious to know what sex with him would be like since we aren't in love. I wonder if I'd like it or if it would fall flat because I don't feel love for him. "If I said that I wanted you to please me, how would you do it?"

Kieran gets up and tugs on my hand. "Come with me." I stand, and he leads me away from the sitting area toward his bed. "I'm going to show you how I would do it."

Oh no. "I meant in a hypothetical situation. Not the real thing."

"We're not going to have sex. But you asked a question, and I'm going to give you an answer."

He stops when we reach the bed. "Lie down on your back."

No way I'm doing this. "Kieran…"

"Shh… I'm not going to do anything you don't want me to do. I swear…" He grins. "On the life of our firstborn son."

Our firstborn son.

I sit on the side of the bed and slide to the middle, closing my eyes as I lie flat on my back. I press my knees together when I remember that I'm not wearing knickers and wait for whatever will come next. When I consider what I'm doing, I realize it's one of the stupider things I've done in my life—lie on a bed, without knickers, before a man who threatened to rape me.

The bed dips, and I jolt at the same time that my eyes pop open. A second later Kieran's face is hovering above mine, close but our bodies not touching. "The first thing I would do is kiss you. An open-mouthed kiss because I would want to feel your tongue against mine and taste the whisky still lingering there." He moves lower and I feel his warm breath on my skin. "When I finished, I'd kiss your neck beginning at that sensitive spot below your ear, and I'd slowly move downward until I reach your tits." Kieran moves lower so his face lingers over my chest. "I would suck this one first and roll my tongue around your nipple while I squeezed the other with my hand and used my thumb to make your nipple hard."

Strange sensations fire from my nipples down to my lower groin. I tense and relax the muscles inside my body… down there. Even the act of breathing becomes more pronounced. More intentional.

His face poises over my lower abdomen. "My mouth would never leave your skin as I kiss your stomach and think about putting a baby inside you."

Oh. Fuck.

"When I finished here, I would spread your legs apart. I'd go down and bury my face between your legs and lick and suck until you come all over my face and scream my name. And when you were completely and utterly spent from coming, I would push my cock inside you and fill your womb with my seed, hopefully putting our firstborn son inside you."

Oh.

Fuck.

Me.

"Do you think you would want me to do any of those things to you?"

I lift my head off the bed and our eyes meet, my mouth agape. My breath panting. I squirm and the top of my groin, covered only by a thin layer of silk, brushes against him.

He moves to kneel on the bed beside me and pulls my bunched gown away from where it has gathered between my legs. "Judging by the looks of this silk, someone's pussy is drenching wet. I bet all it would take is my blowing my breath on your cunt to make you orgasm."

No man has ever said anything like that to me. Not a single one of The Fellowship brothers would have dared. "You are crude."

"And you are horny."

He isn't wrong, but he's ill-mannered for pointing it out so blatantly. I kick at him with my foot. "Your mouth is vulgar."

He chuckles and catches my ankle, pulling me down the bed so he's kneeling between my legs. "Don't be embarrassed. I'm happy that I was able to make you wet so easily. That's a very good indication that we're compatible, at least sexually. Most people in arranged marriages aren't."

How is it possible that I want him to do all of those things he just described while I also want to kick him in his balls?

"Say yes, and I'll make you a very happy woman." His fingers creep up my inner thigh. "Starting right now."

I push his hand away. "The promise of an orgasm won't make me say yes to your marriage proposal."

"What will? Because I very much want you to say yes."

This isn't a date we're talking about. Or even a hookup. This is marriage. The forever kind where you don't get to divorce if things don't go well. "I need time to think about it."

"How long do you need?"

I don't like being rushed, especially when it's something this important. "I'll know when I know."

"We don't have forever. I'll need you to be prompt with your decision." This man is so damn pushy.

He unbuttons his top button and then the second and third. "What are you doing?"

"Getting ready for bed." He continues unbuttoning.

"You're going to sleep here?"

He chuckles. "Aye, this is my bed."

I can't stay with this man. "Where will I sleep?"

"Right there, in my bed with me."

"Are you crazy? We can't do that." My voice rises a few octaves.

"We can, and we will."

"I haven't said yes to marrying you."

"I didn't dissolve our prior agreement. Those terms still apply."

"But you proposed." And spoke sweetly to me.

"Either our earlier agreement or our engagement is in effect. Which is it?"

"I'm either your captive or your fiancée?"

"That's it exactly."

He wins either way. "I haven't accepted your proposal, so I guess that makes me your captive."

He sheds his shirt and tosses it on the bench at the foot of the bed. "I sleep in the nude." He unbuckles his belt and I look away. His pants and some form of black underpants join his shirt on the bench. "Look at me."

I suck my bottom lip, hesitating a moment before turning so that my eyes can meet his.

"Look at my cock, Westlyn."

I suck my lip harder and do as he tells me. Not because I'm being a good little girl who wants to obey her captor's orders. I do it for me, because curiosity is eating me alive. I want to see what a real-life cock looks like.

"You see this? How hard I am? That's what you do to me because I want you so badly."

No man has ever told me that he wants me. No man has ever shown me his erection and then said that I was the reason behind it. No man has ever made me feel this desirable. I don't hate knowing that I have the power to do that to Kieran Hendry, even if he is an asshole.

He goes into the bathroom, leaving the door open. The bastard wants me to hear him jerk off. And I do.

Slapping. Smacking. Spanking.

Groans. Growls. Grunts.

All of the sounds carry directly from the bathroom to my ears. And I want to reach between my legs so badly. "Uhh, West…lyn." I swear I nearly orgasm when I hear the way my name sounds coming from his lips when he comes.

He emerges from the bathroom and climbs into bed beside me. "Get under the covers."

I lift my bum and push the linens down. I'm taken by surprise when he grabs me around my waist and pulls me against him with my back against his front. Damn silk gown makes me glide across the bed like a pat of butter over a hot piece of bread. "I want to feel my wife against me tonight, and I don't want to hear any of your cheeky shite about it."

"I'm not your—"

"Not another word, Westlyn, or my cock will become your muzzle."

"Asshole," I whisper.

"What was that?" I lean as far as I can away from him while being held around my waist and say nothing. "That's what I thought. Now go to sleep."

Not likely.

CHAPTER FIVE

KIERAN HENDRY

I WAKE to a beautiful woman wrapped around me. Not the position we started out in last night, but I like this one too. Maybe more, since her knee is bent and her leg is wrapped around my torso with my hard cock pressing against the split of her pussy.

Fuck. It's right there against her entrance. How am I supposed to resist pushing it inside her?

I move my hips forward and press the head against her slit, making it slip between her lips. One thrust and I'd slide into her tight virginal hole. It would feel so fucking good.

I want to.

Fuck, I want to.

But I can't.

I can't let Westlyn leave here without being claimed, but it can't happen like this. She'd hate me forever, and that's not the way I want to begin my marriage.

"Westlyn." She doesn't stir so I say her name a second time. Her eyes flutter open, and she rapidly blinks several times. I anticipate her jerking away from me the second her brain registers the position we're in. But she doesn't. Instead, her eyes focus on mine. "Careful. I have a very limited amount of restraint right now."

Her hips pull back, but then she thrusts them forward so the tip of my cock rubs between her upper lips. She does it again. And again. And again. "Not kidding, Westlyn. You're pushing me too far, and I'm running out of control. You have to stop rubbing your pussy on me if we're not going to fuck."

She stills her hips and closes her eyes. "I shouldn't have done that but... it just feels so good."

"I can make you feel good, so fucking good, but first you have to tell me that you'll be my wife."

She shakes her head. "I'm not ready to do that."

"It's going to happen." I lift her hand and wrap her fingers around mine so the engagement ring is visible. "You didn't take this ring off because you know you're going to marry me."

"I haven't made up my mind."

"I think you need a little help deciding." I push my hand between our bodies until my fingers reach her slick center.

She grabs my wrist and shakes her head. "No, Kieran."

"I'm only going to touch on the outside. I won't push my fingers in."

"Kieran…"

"Let me give you what you need. I promise you'll be able to see more clearly after you come." Clearly see that you should say yes to my proposal.

"We both know this isn't supposed to happen until you claim me."

"You're the only thing preventing that. I'll claim you right now if you'll let me." I press a soft kiss to her lips and toy with her bottom lip by sucking it into my mouth and releasing it. She tilts her hips forward and I push my finger through her wet slit. Once my finger is well coated with her natural lubrication, I move it to her clit and rub it side to side over the tiny erect nub. "Your pussy is so wet. I want to taste it."

Westlyn presses her forehead to mine and tightens her grip on my upper arms. "Oh God. That feels so good. Don't stop."

Her breathing increases, and she wraps her hand around my cock. "I want us to come together."

"Uhh… fuck." I open my eyes and jolt when I see the back of West-lyn's head. Because she's lying on her side, her back turned to me. Breath deep and steady. Not awake with her hand around my cock.

Fuck, that dream was a cruel joke.

She's in the same position as last night when I pulled her against me with my arm draped over her waist and her bum pressed against my cock. I'm not sure she has moved a muscle in the last seven hours.

Fuck, my dick is hard. I can't continue to be this close to her and not act upon all the things I want to do to her.

I need to shoot something.

I shower and find Westlyn awake and sitting up in bed when I leave the bathroom to choose my suit for the day. Her eyes are red and swollen. She cried last night? I didn't hear a peep from her. "Good morning." Her eyes do a once-over before she looks away from my body covered only by the towel wrapped around my waist. "You can look at me if you want. I don't mind." Her only response is a shake of her head. "I'm going to the shooting range. I'd like it if you came with me." Same response, which is no reply. "I'm very good. Some people enjoy watching me with a gun."

"Why would I want to watch you shoot a gun?"

"Because it would be more interesting than these four walls." And because I'm proud of my skills. I'm eager to show her what I can.

"I want to see Ellison."

"That's not going to happen."

"I don't even know for sure that she's okay."

"I swore to you on our firstborn son's life that no harm would come to her. That's not something I take lightly. I would never break that vow."

"*Our son.* You're very comfortable throwing those two words around."

"Because it's only a matter of time. You're going to give me a son. Hopefully more than one and together they'll one day lead this brotherhood."

"So stuck on having a boy. Why a son? A daughter is just as capable of leading."

I can see what a strong woman Westlyn is. I'm not surprised that she'd call me out on this.

"I don't disagree, but my daughters will be precious to me in a way that differs from my sons. I would never let them be placed in harm's way."

"How do you know that you'll have separate feelings about your girls? Won't you love your children equally?"

"I will, but I feel very differently about my sister than I do my brothers. I think the same would be true for my sons and daughters."

"You're using plurals when you talk about both genders. How many kids do you want to have?"

I like that we're discussing children. I don't think we'd be doing that if she were planning to turn down my proposal. "I don't know. Several."

"A couple is two. A few is three. I consider several to be four or more."

"Minimum of four." Probably more, but I don't want to frighten her.

Her eyes widen. "You expect me to carry and give birth to that many bairns?"

"Of course. And I plan on putting the first one in your belly as soon as possible."

"I wouldn't have a say about that?"

Westlyn grew up in a brotherhood. She knows this is how we do things. "It's what will be expected of us by both brotherhoods. We're obligated to quickly bind our union. You're aware of our practices."

"I am, but it's so archaic. I thought that maybe you wanted something less… old-fashioned."

"This is our life. We are a people of tradition and this is one of them. Marriage treaties and the babies resulting from those unions bring brotherhoods together in harmony. They establish peace when nothing else will. Wouldn't it be a wonderful thing to tell our children one day that the brotherhood they've grown up in and their mother's brotherhood were once at war, but our marriage and their existence brought peace to the two of them?"

"I've never known peace. We've been at war with The Order since before I was born. There's never been a time when I wasn't in danger. I don't want that for my children. I don't want that for anyone's children."

"It's another reason that makes your marrying me the right choice." She doesn't have an argument for that.

"Since you haven't agreed to marry me, our prior agreement is still intact. That means you're going to the shooting range with me, and you aren't going to put up a fight about it. Get up and shower."

She grasps her white silk gown. "And wear what? This?"

"My wife will never be looked upon by any brother while wearing something like that."

"Are you going to keep calling me your wife although we're not even engaged?"

"Hold up your left hand and look at your ring finger." Her lips press together in a tight line, but she does as I order. "You're wearing the engagement ring I placed on your finger last night. You could have taken it off, but you didn't. We're engaged. Now get up and shower."

Westlyn tugs at the neckline of her gown, pulling it up to cover her cleavage. I love her chaste behavior. It actually turns me the fuck on. "Will Mrs. Bruce be back to help me dress?"

"No. She'll be preparing our breakfast while you get ready." I think Westlyn may misunderstand Nan's role. "I had her come to help you last night because it was supposed to be a special event. She only helps the Hendry women prepare for important occasions."

"You didn't tell me what I'll be wearing today."

I suppose I didn't. "You have new clothes hanging in the closet. I suggest that you choose something warm. There's a cold front moving in. Probably going to get snow later today."

"Who bought the clothes for me?"

"My mother." And she was happy to do so. She's very excited about my taking a wife.

Westlyn touches the plunging neckline of her gown again. "Did she choose this as well?"

"Aye."

"She picked it for a virgin who was being claimed by her mate."

I think she understands now. "Aye."

"It's lovely."

"She chose your intimates. I chose your lingerie." And I'm eager to see her wear it.

"Lingerie?"

"Yes, and not all of it is intended for a virgin." I like the sweet stuff, but I also like naughty. Some of the pieces I chose for Westlyn are sexy as fuck.

Her eyes widen. "Oh."

"Would you like to meet my mum? Maybe talk to her about her experience as a treaty bride?"

"I would love to talk to your mother."

I'm glad to see how eager she is to meet her mother-in-law. "I'll introduce you after we get back from the shooting range."

UNINTENDED

Westlyn looks at the towel around my waist. "Are you finished in the bathroom?"

"Aye."

She watches me as she slides off the side of the bed, and I smile when she dashes to the bathroom and shuts the door with a loud thud. Well, I wanted an inexperienced virgin. I got one. A very timid one.

Westlyn has gone her entire life without sex. She must be horny as fuck. How could she not be? "How old are you?" I call out to her through the door. Can't believe I didn't ask that when I was considering which woman I'd take for a wife.

"Twenty-three."

Untouched for twenty-fucking-three years. Bet her toes curl in under thirty seconds the first time I put my hands on her. Giving Westlyn her first orgasm, hearing her moan with ecstasy for the first time... it's going to be so much fun.

"How old are you?" she calls out.

I open the door. "Twenty-eight."

"What are you doing?"

She's already in the shower, but I have a clear view of her through the glass despite her hands being used as a shield to hide from me. Small waist. Curvy hips and thighs. Full breasts spilling over the top of her hand. I am not disappointed. And I'm tempted as fuck to drop my towel and get into the shower with her.

"I don't want to continue speaking to you through the door."

"Then you shouldn't have called out and initiated the conversation. Get out."

"You don't think a man has the right to look at the woman who belongs to him?"

"Even if I say yes to your marriage proposal, I won't *belong* to you. I am my own person."

She's delusional if she believes that misconception. "That's where you're wrong, Westlyn. When you take my name and my cock, you will become mine... my property. But that also means you'll become my treasure to protect. I will place myself between you and whatever danger presents itself. No harm will ever come to you or our children. That's my vow to you."

She stares at me for a minute before dropping her hands, giving me an unobstructed view of her naked body. I'm not sure what it means, but fuck, I take advantage of what she has on display; this woman is gorgeous. Everything from the top of her head to the tips of her pink toenails is perfect. She's exactly what I would have chosen in a mate.

I feel my dick beginning to harden, and I don't want to go there. Not again, when I know she'll offer no relief; my cock doesn't want my hand. "I'll wait for you out there."

"All right."

I'm not certain because the glass is fogging up, but I think I see a smirk on her face. I'd love to kiss it off and replace it with a mouth agape, begging me to give her more.

It's going to happen, Westlyn Breckenridge Hendry. It's only a matter of time.

CHAPTER SIX

WESTLYN BRECKENRIDGE

A BROAD SMILE spreads across Mrs. Bruce's face when Kieran and I come into the kitchen. "Good mornin', Nan."

Her face lights up when Kieran kisses her cheek. The affection I see between the two is surprising. "I didn't expect you to be up so early this mornin'."

"Tried to sleep in, but my doll wouldn't let me."

"First of all, don't call me your doll. And second, I didn't do anything to keep you from sleeping."

"Trust me. Even if you were unaware, you definitely did... *keep me up*."

My cheeks warm and pulsate; I can't believe he said something so blatantly cheeky in front of this sweet old lady.

"Come to the table. Both of you need a hearty breakfast to restore your energy."

I wonder exactly what it is Mrs. Bruce believes we did last night to need all of this restoration of energy.

Kieran pulls out the seat left of the captain's chair at the end of the table. "You will always sit and stand to my left."

Another ridiculous archaic tradition? "Haven't you heard of gender equality? Women can sit and stand wherever they like."

"You will sit to my left. You will stand to my left. You will sleep to my left... unless we are in a bed where the door is to the left. In that case, you will sleep to my right. It's imperative that you are always positioned where I can best defend you if we are attacked. Because I'm right-handed. Not because I'm trying to suppress your gender."

How was I to know that he wasn't trying to define my gender role by placing me to his left? "Well, you should have just said so."

"I didn't think I had to. Didn't your father have your mother stand to his non-dominant side?"

I can say one thing for Kieran. He will be adamant about protecting me if I become his wife… just as a husband should be. I liked what he said while I was in the shower. Not the part about my being his property. I liked him saying that I would be his treasure to protect and that he would place himself between me and whatever danger was presented. And that no harm would ever come to me or our children.

His drive to keep me safe is sexy. Very sexy.

I didn't see that protective nature in my father, and it's shameful to admit. "My father wasn't concerned with protecting anyone but himself. He was a real jackass."

"I never met your father, but I've heard many things about him."

I'm sure that nothing he heard was good. "You didn't miss out on anything except evil incarnate."

"He was killed by Sinclair, his own nephew. That tells me a lot about Abram."

"My cousin didn't have a choice. My father told Sin that he was going to kill his twin sons and then join The Order to lead the fight against The Fellowship." I've never told anyone about my father's heinous threats to murder those innocent babies; he brought so much shame upon our family.

"Your father should have been killed. Probably sooner than he was."

"He was evil, and I fully understand that, but I could never bring myself to hate him because he never mistreated me. I think he loved me the only way he knew how."

"What about your mother? I'm curious to know what kind of woman marries a man like Abram Breckenridge?"

"A power-hungry one."

"She should have married Thane if it was power she wanted."

"It was mortifying to have the overbearing parents who walked around acting as though they should be the ones leading the brother-hood. Completely disrespectful. Thane was too kind to my father. It took a lot of work and patience on his part to keep Dad at bay, but he did it because he loved his brother."

"I'm sure Thane has taken responsibility for your mum?"

"Yes, but not because he wanted to. He felt it was his duty, but that doesn't mean he or Isobel are going to tolerate her shite. Believe me when I say that she pushes them to their limits, just as my dad did."

"Isobel told me you were being saved for someone?"

"My father wanted me to marry Sin."

I see the same puzzled look on Kieran's face that I've seen on everyone else's when they hear what my father was planning. "Your relation is too close for marriage."

"Technically, no. My father was adopted so we aren't genetically tied, but that never mattered to either of us. Sin and I are cousins. We were raised together. I could never think of him in any other way, blood relation or not."

"I guess if Abram couldn't be leader of The Fellowship, marrying you to Sinclair was his next best option. But why you and not your sister? She's older."

"He never said why, but I think it's because he saw me as a better puppet. Evanna has been too selfish and spoiled to concern herself with Fellowship business. She wouldn't have carried out his instructions because she'd have been too busy shopping or having her nails done." My sister has been high maintenance in the past, but I've seen a change in her since she fell in love with Craig. He doesn't have the money or status to maintain the luxurious lifestyle she's been accustomed to. But she doesn't care, which makes me so proud of her.

"Further evidence that you are the one I want."

No man has ever spoken to me the way Kieran does. Telling me that I'm beautiful and that he wants me and that I'm going to be his. Feeling desired and wanted… it's intoxicating, even if it is coming from this brute. It's a nice change from being ignored by Fellowship men.

Kieran looks at my plate. "You need to eat to replenish your strength so Nan doesn't figure out that we didn't fuck all night."

Bleu says that Sin's mouth is filthy when they're behind closed doors. Ellison says the same about Jamie, but this crude language coming from a man is new to me.

"And after I ate all of those oysters to get my *womanly juices flowing*." I close my eyes and regret the words the moment they leave my mouth.

Kieran chuckles. "That was me who got your womanly juices flowing, doll. Not the oysters."

"I should have known that you'd be crass and bring that up."

"It wasn't me who brought up your womanly juices."

Dammit. He's got me there. I walked right into that one because my tongue got ahead of my brain. I should change the subject to something else he'd be interested in discussing.

I hold up my hand and spread my fingers. "This really is a gorgeous ring."

"Gorgeous ring for a gorgeous girl."

I knew that would change the direction of our conversation. "No one would ever look at my hand and wonder if I'm taken."

"A definite warning sign for other men to fuck off." He reaches for my hand and looks at the ring. I think he really likes seeing it on me. "I will end any man who doesn't heed this warning."

I think he means that.

We finish breakfast and Kieran leads me across the property to another building. "This is my private indoor range. I'm the only person who shoots here. I thought you might prefer it over outdoor shooting since it's so cold today."

"I appreciate that. I'd probably make you miss your target because my teeth would be chattering so hard."

"I never miss my target. My accuracy is spot-on."

I haven't practiced lately. "My accuracy is *not* spot-on."

"You shoot?"

That caught his attention. I nod. "I do, but I'm not the best."

"It isn't possible for you to be the best because *I'm* the best." Kieran isn't all serious, all the time. I like this lighter side of him.

"Cocky much?"

He chuckles. "I'm very cocky when it comes to shooting a gun."

"I think you're cocky about more than shooting."

"Won't argue with you."

I follow Kieran to a bay and he crosses one arm over his midsection. He pulls a handgun from a holster and then repeats the action on the opposite side. I did not see that coming. "I had no idea that you had those guns on you."

"I always have guns on me. Always… unless I'm naked. But even then, they aren't far from my reach." He uses his finger to beckon me. I go to him, and he places a pair of safety glasses on my face. "Stand here and show me your stance."

I move into the position Bleu taught me. Arms fully extended. Shoulders relaxed. Feet hip-width apart. Knees slightly bent. Upper body leaning forward ever so slightly. Weight balanced. Tight grip on my invisible handgun.

"Very nice, doll. Did Abram teach you?"

"No. Sin's wife, Bleu."

"Ahh… Bleu Breckenridge, the former FBI agent who fell in love with and married her target's son—the next leader of The Fellowship. Only married a year and already breeding the next generation of leaders. *Two* sons and a daughter. That's impressive."

They took in an orphaned baby girl while Bleu was pregnant with the twins. I'm not a bit shocked that Bleu refused to give her up even though she already had two sons of her own on the way. Three babies. It's like having triplets. Bairns moving in three different directions at once. I don't know how she does it. I also don't know how she could want more, but she does. "Their story is an unlikely romance."

"As unlikely as the captive who falls in love with her captor? Or the wife in the arranged marriage who falls in love with her husband?"

I could never fall in love with him—the leader of The Order. The man who kidnapped me. The man who threatened to do whatever he wanted with my body against my will. But I can't let him know that. "I suppose stranger things have happened."

Kieran holds up one of his handguns. "What kind of gun did you shoot when you were taught?"

"Beretta." Bleu's gun of choice.

"Both of these are heavier and more powerful, but this one will feel more like a Beretta in your hands."

I take Kieran's gun and wrap my hand around it the way Bleu taught me. "Definitely heavier."

"The recoil is going to be stronger than a Beretta, so you must grip it tightly."

I lift my arms and relax my shoulders. "I have a tight grip."

"Set your sights on your target. Visually align it." I nod. "Stop nodding. You'll lose your alignment."

I'm getting tired of being bossed around by this man. "Stop annoying me."

"Your smart mouth is going to get you into a heap of trouble with me. Keep on and you might find yourself across my lap getting spanked."

I should keep my mouth shut and not provoke him, but doing so does something to me. I can't resist poking this bear. "That's amusing. Maybe you can be a comedian if this Order thing doesn't work out for you."

"I'd spank you right now if you weren't holding my gun."

"You'd like that, wouldn't you?"

"I'd like it far more than you know."

I bet he would. He's probably into all kinds of kinky and sadistic things. He looks like the type. And I bet the foolish women of The Syndicate and The Order would let him do whatever he likes.

"Are you ready for your ear protection?"

"Please. Maybe then I won't have to listen to you yammer on."

"Your arse is going to make the acquaintance of my palm tonight."

I'm looking ahead, so I can't see his expression, but I slightly panic until I hear the light chuckle that follows.

Playful Kieran. He's much more pleasant than vile Kieran. "You don't scare me."

He leans close so his mouth hovers over my ear. "I'm going to make you regret saying that, later tonight."

I take my eyes off the target and turn to look at him over my shoulder. "Careful. I haven't made my decision about the proposal yet."

"We both know you have." He lifts the protective earmuffs and stretches them over my head. "This is an extended magazine. You have twenty-two rounds."

"Got it."

He lowers the earmuffs over my ears and I resume my stance, visually aligning the center of the paper target. I fire the first shot, completely unprepared for the rearward force that pushes me off-balance, forcing my back to collide with Kieran's front. He removes my earmuffs, and I hear him laughing. "I warned you, doll."

"Shite. That is powerful."

"You're a wee one, so that's a lot of kickback for your small upper body to handle. Does the power frighten you?"

It does a little, but I'll never let him know. I can't ever let him see me cower. "No."

"Want to fire it again?"

"Yes."

Kieran places one hand on my lower abdomen and the other on my upper back, pushing me into position. His hand on my stomach makes all of those exciting tingles I had last night return. Dammit. I hate this man. That shouldn't be happening.

"You need to balance your body in a more forward position for this weapon." I shift and he uses his hands to adjust my body. "Still not quite right."

He moves behind me, wrapping his arms around my body and putting his hands on top of mine. His front presses against my back, forcing my body into the firing position. I feel his breath against my ear before I hear his voice. "You're perfect." His mouth grazes my earlobe and chills erupt down my body. "Don't. Move."

He replaces the protective gear over my ears, and I hesitate a moment before firing over and over until the magazine is empty. Incredible. The force behind this weapon is electrifying. Makes me feel powerful. Brave. Invincible.

I place the gun on the table inside the bay and remove my earmuffs. "That gun does not play."

He takes the earmuffs from me and tosses them next to the gun. He advances and I retreat until my back is pressed against the wall of the bay. Trapped. "Watching you fire off those rounds… it was hot."

Men will use any excuse for being horny. "All I did was shoot a gun."

He shakes his head. "It was so much more than just firing a weapon." I hear the sincerity in his voice. See it in his eyes.

"What does that mean?" And why does it seem to be so important to him?

"You handled my gun with confidence. You fired it with skill. No fear. No hesitation." His hands cup the bottom of my face. He leans in, pressing a soft kiss to my mouth. "It pleases me greatly to see those qualities in my wife."

I don't know if it's his hands touching my face or his lips against mine or hearing him call me his wife, but something makes those damn tingles in my pelvis return. The same ones that made me wet last night. Thank fuck I'm wearing pants.

Kieran Hendry makes me feel like a woman. A desired woman. His words, the way he looks at me, his body language. Everything he does is a huge turn-on. Yet I hate this man. Loathe him. But damn, he has a way of touching me that makes me forget every logical thought in my head. It doesn't make sense to me how I can despise him and at the same time respond so strongly to his touch.

It's my body reacting to him, not my head. It must be hormones and sex drive. Those two things combined have the power to make people do things they wouldn't normally do.

"You're trembling." He grazes the back of his fingers down my cheek and my stomach does some kind of flip. "Do I frighten you?"

I look away because I can't tell him that it isn't fear giving me the trembles.

He grasps my chin and forces me to look at him. "Do. I. Frighten. You?"

"No."

He rubs my bottom lip with his thumb. "Then what is it?"

I shake my head.

He leans in for another kiss but stops before his lips touch mine. We're so close I can feel his breath on my mouth. Just like last night when my body turned to mush.

I'm quivering and my breath has become more rapid. I may even be a little lightheaded.

His bottom lip grazes mine, but he still doesn't kiss me. "I'll back off right now if it's what you want."

I don't want him to back off. I also don't want him to know that I don't want him to back off. Feels too much like giving in to something I'm not supposed to crave.

"I'm going to kiss you."

I'm his captive. We made an agreement. I must submit without a fight per our deal to maintain Ellison's safety.

Yeah. Keep telling yourself that, Wes. Maybe if you say it enough, you'll start to believe it.

His fingers lace through my hair and he holds me prisoner when he lowers his mouth to mine. I open, giving his tongue an invitation to come inside. The two meet, and together they become erotic dance partners with Kieran taking the lead.

I've only had one very forgettable kiss in my life. But this kiss... I could live a million years and never forget it or the way I feel right now.

He stops, his lips hovering over mine. His breath warm against my skin. "More or stop? Your decision."

He's asking me to venture further with him. My body says yes, but my head tells me that one more step will take me to a place I shouldn't go with this man. I'm twenty-three and being kissed for the second time in my life. I don't want this to stop. "More."

His mouth drags across my jaw, leaving kisses in its path. It travels down the side of my neck and I tilt my head, offering him full access. Submitting.

I close my eyes and debate what the hell I'm doing. Kieran asked for my permission. Not my submission. I said yes when I didn't have to.

He pushes his hand under my sweater and grips my lower back, pulling me against him. "More?" He doesn't have to have permission to do any of this to me. I'm his captive to do with as he wishes, and no one will stop him. Yet he's asking for my consent.

"Yes."

He pins me against the wall with his hips. I'm trapped with no escape. I should be panicking, but I'm not.

I have no idea what I'm doing. I only know that I like what's happening between us more than I should.

His mouth migrates as low as it can until the neck of my sweater won't allow him to go any lower. And despite my lack of experience at making out, I know what's coming next. This man isn't going to let a sweater get in his way.

My chest heaves up and down, my breathing loud. I'm shocked by the sudden and unexpected urgency I feel for Kieran. I ignore the warnings I hear inside my head telling me to stop.

His hand is moving to my breasts just as I anticipated, but I still jolt when his thumb rubs my nipple through the fabric of my bra.

"I can't wait to have you under me. I'm going to make you come so hard. Over and over and over." My light gasp makes him chuckle. "You're going to love all the things I make your body feel."

The touching. The kissing. The promises. All of it pools like pure liquid seduction between my legs, my body's invitation for Kieran to keep going.

"You want that, don't you? To feel passion and ecstasy and pleasure?"

Fuck. Yes.

I want that.

I jolt when I hear someone clearing his voice, but Kieran simply removes his hand from my sweater and backs away. He inhales deeply and exhales slowly. "Go the fuck away. Now, if you don't want to die." His jaw is clenched, and there's a touch of growl to his voice.

"My apologies, Mr. Hendry. Your father sent me to get you."

Kieran stands tall and adjusts his tie. "Where is my father?"

"Waiting for you in the car, sir."

I think this means they're leaving the compound. Something must be happening. Maybe they're going to meet with The Fellowship Council again. Maybe I'm about to leave this place.

Kieran cradles my face and kisses my forehead, just as I've seen Sin do with Bleu a thousand times. It feels very affectionate. I like it.

"Escort Miss Breckenridge back to my quarters."

This Kieran is not the Kieran I met last night. This one is showing me respect. This one is working for my affection. This one is trying to win my heart.

But after last night, it may be too little, too late.

CHAPTER SEVEN

KIERAN HENDRY

WORST TIMING EVER.

I was making progress with Westlyn. She's bending. Every minute we spend together, I can feel it happening more and more. She's going to say yes soon.

I'm very happy about where she and I are, but I'm concerned about what's going on. Something must have gone sideways. My father would never pull me away from Westlyn at this pivotal moment for no good reason.

I get into the car and my father gives Niall the signal to drive. "I'm sorry to interrupt your time with Westlyn, but we have a problem."

"I assume it's the kind of problem that only I can solve?"

"Aye. We've had a wrench thrown into our plan. His name is William Walker, and he's currently gathering supporters to start a revolt. He's trying to convince brothers to overthrow us before we can carry out the marriage treaty exchange."

This I take fucking personally. It directly affects my mate and me. This isn't a forgivable offense to commit against your leaders.

The brothers of The Order don't know us. They don't understand our ways... but they're going to. And it's going to be a lesson well learned. Not one of them will question why we are called the sleeping giants when I'm finished ridding us of this wrench.

I reach for the hard case containing my M24 and pop the latches. I take out the rifle and begin the drill of preparing my weapon for my next assassination. "Where are we going?"

"Walker and four others are meeting in one of our warehouses right now."

"Good. They'll be wide open with limited options for cover. Am I killing all of them?" I place five rounds in the magazine. One bullet for each man committing treason against us. No extras needed. I never miss.

"Leave one alive. A witness who can tell everyone what happens when you commit treason against a Hendry."

"Yes, sir." This rifle and I have been a pair for thirteen years. We've taken down many fierce brothers and many cowards together. "Does it matter which one survives?"

"No. Just as long as it's not Walker. He dies first."

I finish the drill and place my M24 on my lap.

"Have you had Westlyn yet?"

"No, but I think we're moving in that direction. I was in the middle of making progress when your man came to get me."

"I didn't want to interrupt what little time you have with her, but I had no choice. We have to act now."

"I understand, and I agree."

"You can't let Westlyn leave the compound without bedding her."

"I know, and I'm working to gain her consent. I don't want to do it by force." I hope it doesn't come to that. I don't know Westlyn well, but I'm certain that she'd hate me forever if I claimed her by force.

"Consensual is best, but I can't stress to you how important it is that you bind your union as quickly as possible."

"I'm aware."

"Care for a bit of advice from your old man?"

"Aye."

"You're twenty-eight years old and in a position of power. I'm certain you've had plenty of women by now and need no advice on the act itself, but this time will be different from any other time you've been with a woman. None of the ones before now have been your virginal wife. You're claiming a woman for the first time, but you're also trying to get her pregnant. This won't be like any experience you've ever had."

"I've never had a virgin. Never been inside a woman bare. Or came inside one either." I knew from an early age never to have unprotected sex even if I thought I felt some kind of affection for my lover. Not that I've ever had anything more than a hard-on for any woman.

"There's nothing else in the world like it."

"I'm hopeful that it will happen tonight." She was giving me all the right signals before we were interrupted.

"She's going to be nervous. You should share a few glasses of whisky together to calm her nerves. Once she loosens up, begin slowly and pleasure her until she orgasms. This will make her body less tense when you take her. Be gentle and use this first time to focus on pleasuring her instead of yourself. If you make it good for her, she'll be eager to do it again."

I know how to make a woman come, but I've never been overly concerned with making it happen. I've been more interested in receiving pleasure than giving it. But sex with Westlyn will be focused on what her body needs for satisfaction. In a way, this will be a first for me too.

"Find out where she is in her cycle. If it's been around two weeks since the start of her last period, the timing could be right for you to conceive. Go as deep as she'll let you and, for good measure, keep her in bed for a while afterward."

My father has five children. I'm inclined to think that he knows what works best.

"Are you ready to be a grandfather, old man?" My father isn't old, but I like calling him that.

"I am. It'll be nice to have bairns around the house again. And God knows it'll make your mum happy. Are you prepared to be a husband and father?"

"I am." I don't know Westlyn, but time will fix that. And I don't love her, but I think time could fix that as well if she's open to it. I'm keen to find out what our future holds.

The car comes to a stop in front of the warehouse. "I'm giving you a three-minute head start to enter through the back door before I go in through the front."

"Why go in at all? I can take care of it by myself."

"Being present for these hits sends a message. Sitting in the car ensuring that my suit isn't splattered with blood achieves nothing."

My father makes an excellent point. "Do you want to say anything before I start taking them out?"

"No. All they need to do is see my face. When only one remains, that's when I'll talk."

"Got it."

I enter the back of the warehouse and hear voices toward the front of the building.

"These motherfuckers don't have the right to come in here and take over. They've never been part of The Order. Who the fuck are they to think they know what is best for our brotherhood? The Fellowship killed our leader. We can't let that go. They must be made to bleed."

My father wasn't wrong. This is the makings of a revolt, and it must be stopped before it starts.

I go down on one knee and sit back on my lower leg and foot, using my opposite knee and thigh as a prop to steady my arm and sniper. I use my scope to zero in on the speaker since I'm certain he must be William Walker.

I'm only about a hundred meters away, much closer than usual. This short distance isn't going to leave a pretty corpse. Things are going to be messy. My father will probably have more than blood splattered on his suit.

"They have one of Abram Breckenridge's daughters at the compound right now. The oldest son plans to marry the Fellowship whore and breed little bastards to lead our children and grandchildren. We can't let this happen." He briefly pauses. *"The first thing we have to do is kill the Breckenridge girl."*

Anger. Fury. Rage. They all rise from the pit of my stomach when I hear this man threaten my mate. And I'm suddenly very pleased to be the one taking down this motherfucker.

My father nears and the man stops talking when he sees him. My cue.

I pull the trigger and the bullet enters the center of his forehead. He falls to the ground, and the other four men look around the warehouse, searching for the source of the shot. The first one gets up to run, and I put a bullet through the back of his head. Two more run, and they meet the same fate.

The final man remains in his seat looking at my father. I can see that they're exchanging words, but I can't hear what they are from this distance. Doesn't matter as long as he gets the message and tells the other Order members. No one will overthrow my family or me. It is our birthright to lead this brotherhood, and we are here to stay as are my children, the ones I will have with Westlyn Breckenridge.

I'm already waiting in the backseat when my father returns to the car.

He reaches into his pocket and takes out a handkerchief, wiping the blood and other gore from his face. "It isn't possible for that message to be misinterpreted. Hopefully that will put an end to any more of this nonsense."

"I heard them say that they were going to kill Westlyn." I'm surprised by the feelings I had when I heard their threats against her. Of course, it angered me because they were talking about bringing harm to something that belongs to me, but it was more than that. I feared for her safety.

"Aye, I heard as well. But they're dead now. No worries. They can't harm her."

"One of them still lives." He could plant ideas in others' heads about killing Westlyn.

"The man's a coward. He didn't run because he was frozen with fear. Bastard pissed himself. He isn't going to be part of any rebellion again."

"Is it abnormal to already worry for Westlyn's safety?"

"You've accepted her as your future. I don't think it's abnormal at all. And as you come to know her, your drive to protect her is only going to grow."

I was so angry when my father told me that I had to marry a Fellowship woman. I didn't think it could ever feel like anything more than hatred and bitterness and resentment. My strong need to protect her is unexpected.

The uneasy feeling in my stomach is alleviated when I enter my bedroom and find Westlyn napping on the couch. Safe and sound. She's lying on her side, knees bent with one arm under her head, her brown and golden hair spilling over the edge of the couch.

I go to her and crouch low so that our faces are almost level. Her skin is creamy and unblemished except for a small white scar on her chin. It's the first time I've noticed it. Wonder what happened.

I can't resist twirling a lock of her hair around my finger. So soft and silky. Exactly the kind of hair that should belong to a princess. My Mafia princess.

Her eyes open, and she blinks rapidly several times before smiling. Smiling as though she's pleased to see me. Not pulling away out of fear or contempt. "You were gone a long time."

"I'm sorry about that." The disposal of those bodies took much

GEORGIA CATES

longer than anticipated.

"Where did you go?"

"To tend to Order business."

"Did that business involve meeting with The Fellowship council?"

"No."

"Oh."

I hear disappointment in her voice. I stand and remove my jacket and gun harness, placing both on the cocktail table. "Scoot back." I lie on the couch beside Westlyn, my front touching hers, with my arm draped over her body. I press my forehead to hers and close my eyes. "Let's just lie like this for a while and forget The Order, The Fellowship, and all the filthy things we're forced to do even when we don't want to."

"Kieran?" Her voice is barely more than a whisper.

"Mmm… hmm?"

"Did something bad happen while you were gone?"

Westlyn has no idea that I've committed the worst of the worst. She doesn't know that it reduces me to a broken mess. No one does, because I always retreat afterward. It's what I do so that my weakness isn't revealed. "Yes, doll. Something very bad happened, and I need to shut everything off for a little while."

"Okay."

That's all she says, and she doesn't know how grateful I am that she doesn't press for more information. I'm not ready to have that talk.

I've taken four more lives today. I used to believe that killing would become easier. It hasn't. These men, despite the numerous reasons they gave me for taking their lives… they had families. Parents, wives, children, grandchildren.

I don't enjoy being an assassin, but it's who I am. Killing is my contribution to my brotherhood; I protect my brothers. And I protect what is mine.

I pull Westlyn against me and hold her tightly. Her touch is consoling, comforting, even healing. I didn't know that this solace was what I've been missing by not having a mate. I didn't know that it was what I needed in my life. Somebody to lean upon. Somebody to support me when times are hard. Somebody to be here for me.

Maybe somebody to love.

60

CHAPTER EIGHT
WESTLYN BRECKENRIDGE

KIERAN HENDRY ISN'T UNBREAKABLE. He's hurting. I feel his pain wrapped around me as tangibly as his arms, and only God knows why, but I want to comfort this man. I want to take away his torment.

I freely give him what he asks for. We lie facing one another on the couch, motionless with eyes closed, and silently let the world pass us by. Although he does frighten me, I don't do it because I'm afraid not to. I do it because it's what I want to give him.

He showed me his vulnerable side. And I feel certain that it's a part of himself that he's never shown to another woman. Brothers don't do that.

He touches my cheek, and I open my eyes. "I killed four men today."

Killing is part of our world. I know that brothers do it and often, but none of them have ever spoken to me about it. I'm not sure how I feel about hearing these things.

"They were forming a rebellion against us—my family and I." He pauses a moment. "I heard the leader tell the group that they needed to kill you."

Kill me? What the actual fuck?

I might wonder what I'd ever done to deserve a sentence like that, but I already know the answer: I'm a Breckenridge. Guilty by birth if nothing else.

"I was already going to kill them, but something snapped in me when I heard that fucker threaten your life." Kieran cradles the side of my face and caresses my cheek with his thumb. "I'll never hesitate to kill for you."

I know it's wrong. I shouldn't like hearing him say that he's willing to go to that extreme for me, but I do like it. I like it a lot.

His eyes are locked on mine when I lick my lips and lean forward to press them to his. Just the surface of lips on lips until we simultaneously open and our tongues find one another. I press my palms to his chest and circle his pecs through his shirt, feeling the firm muscle beneath my hands. So hard. So strong. So masculine.

I can't believe how nervous I feel. The butterflies in my stomach are alive and fluttering out of control. Electrifying tingles are bouncing back and forth between my nipples and knees.

Our kiss is slow, seductive, and sultry until Kieran grabs the back of my head and pulls me closer, deepening our kiss. My body has a mind of its own, squirming against his. He rises to a sitting position and pulls me with him, lifting me to sit atop him, my legs straddling his body. I've never been wrapped around a man this way.

His hands move to my bum and his fingertips dig into my hips through my pants. He pulls my body against his and rocks. Hard. Dry humping me. I hold on tightly and move in counterpoint. It's nothing but instinct. And there isn't a single cell in my body that's not on fire for him. "This is wrong," I whisper.

"Doing it isn't wrong when it's with your intended." Kieran gets up from the sofa and holds me around my waist, carrying me from the sitting area to his bed. "I am your intended." He lowers my body to the bed and crawls over me, nestling between my thighs. "Let me claim you, Westlyn. I swear that I will make it so fucking good for you."

This man has flipped a switch inside me. Ice-cold to red-hot. Polar opposites. The war between my body and mind is a crazy and unbeliev-able clash, and I don't know which one is stronger.

Kieran Hendry is a stranger. How is it possible for me to want to give him my body? Hand over a piece of myself to him forever?

"I want to, but..."

He places a finger to my lips. "No buts."

"I can't do this until I've spoken to my family."

Kieran tilts his head and sighs. "That's not going to happen, doll."

"You are a leader. You can make it happen if you want."

"I'm not *the* leader. My father is, and he's made his decision. There will be a marriage treaty between The Order and The Fellowship."

"I'm not saying no. There can still be a treaty, but I want to speak with Thane and Sin before there's no going back."

UNINTENDED

"There's already no going back. You're mine, and I'm not asking for Thane and Sin's permission to take you."

"Forcing their hand this way doesn't seem like a very good way to begin a treaty."

"What do you think Thane and Sin would say if we asked them to hand you over to be my bride?"

The point Kieran is making is a legitimate one. Thane and Sin would never freely give me to them.

"You're not answering because you know I'm right."

"Why propose then? Why make a production of getting down on your knee and giving me your grandmother's ring if I don't have a choice?" I look at the diamond on my finger and wonder if he made up the whole thing about his grandmother. "Did this even belong to her?"

"Yes, it did. And I proposed in a traditional manner because I want this marriage to be real. I want you to marry me because *you* said yes. Not because I claimed you by force and you had no choice."

"I met you last night, not even under half-decent circumstances, and you expect me to sleep with you less than twenty-four hours later so that we'll be bound to one another until death do we part. That's not how normal marriages begin."

"We aren't normal people. They don't write romance novels about our way of life because there's nothing romantic about it. But I'm trying my damnedest because I don't want you to hate me. I want a chance at making this relationship be as normal and real as possible."

I actually believe him. "I appreciate that you're trying, but I need you to be sensitive to the fact that I've been stolen from my home and my people. I'm in a strange place with a man who told me he was going to beat and rape me but now expects me to happily give him my virginity. I need time."

"I want to give you what you need. I swear I do, but my job as leader is to ensure that this treaty happens. That means claiming you before you leave our compound. I have to ensure our union."

I know that Arabella Hendry's loyalty lies with Kieran and this brotherhood, but she's been in my shoes. I hope she can give me encouraging words even if every one coming from her mouth is deceptive. "I want to see your mother."

63

He beams. "That'll make her very happy; she's eager to meet you."

I've just floundered with Kieran on the couch and bed. I'm sure I look a mess. "I need a moment to make myself presentable."

He moves to get up but first leans forward to kiss my forehead. "No worries. You look beautiful."

Dammit. Why can't he just be an asshole all the time? He's giving me whiplash.

I'm a bit fresher and feeling slightly more confident about my appearance when there's a knock at the door. I stand tall and straighten my clothing—the clothes that this woman chose for her anticipated daughter-in-law.

"Come in."

Oh. It's Mrs. Bruce. "Mrs. Hendry is ready to receive Miss Breckenridge."

Silly of me to think Arabella would come to her son's bedroom to talk to me when there's an entire compound.

"Thank you, Nan."

"Would you like me to take her to Mrs. Hendry's sitting room?"

"Thank you, but I think I'll take her."

The sitting room is on the opposite side of the compound, so I get my first look at the interior. It's nothing like my parents' home; my mother has ostentatious taste. Everything in this house has clean lines. I like it. "If this marriage happens, would we live here?"

"This marriage is going to happen, and when it does I'm going to buy you any home you want and shamefully spoil you."

"Another MO for convincing me that this marriage is a good idea?"

"Maybe."

Kieran knocks on a door, and a soft, feminine voice calls out for us to come in. I'm surprised by the woman I see when we enter the sitting room. She looks much too young to have a twenty-eight-year-old son. I also wasn't expecting a fair-haired blonde with pale blue eyes, considering her son's dark hair and eyes. Guess Lennox Hendry must be the dark one of the two.

"Hello, Westlyn." She gets up from the sofa and meets me in the middle of the room. "It's lovely to meet you."

Arabella Grieves Hendry looks nothing like her evil brother, Torrence

Grieves. Her face is youthful, her eyes kind, her smile warm and welcoming. "It's lovely to meet you, Mrs. Hendry."

"None of that Mrs. Hendry stuff. Please… call me Ara."

My brotherhood has been at war with hers for years. It doesn't feel natural to call her by such a personal name.

"I'm sure you're feeling out of sorts, but I'm pleased that you've asked for me." She looks at Kieran. "I think we're all good here. I'll return her to you when we're finished talking."

"Enjoy your girl talk." Kieran goes to his mum and kisses the side of her face before moving closer to whisper something in her ear.

Arabella leans away from him and smiles. "Kieran Bryce…" She smacks his arm. "You are so bad. Get out of here."

Only a few minutes into this meeting and I can already see that Arabella and Kieran have a loving mother-son relationship. Certainly not what you expect to see in a man who killed four men this morning.

He leaves, and his mum goes to her minibar. "I know it's still early, but would you care for a whisky? Might ease your nerves."

"I could stand a drink." Or twelve.

She fills the glass two fingers high, just like every other whisky drinker I know. "The best conversations always begin with whisky."

"That's what I hear although I'm not much of a whisky drinker."

"I only keep the dark stuff. This life calls for it more often than I like. I can send for wine if that's what you prefer."

"No. Whisky is probably the better drink choice for this conversation."

"Probably." She moves to the chair, and I sit across from her on the sofa. She takes a drink of her whisky and looks at me. "You're a very lovely girl."

"Thank you."

"When Nox told Kieran that he had to take you as his wife, he built you up to be some kind of ogre in his mind. Needless to say, he was relieved when he saw you for the first time."

"I'm glad he doesn't find me comparable to an ogre."

"I've never seen my son like this. He's very taken with you, but I'm curious about the way you are feeling toward him."

"I'm puzzled by what I feel." I don't know how to explain what's happening in my head.

"Your body is betraying your head. He touches you and you respond, and you don't know why. Your mind tells you it's wrong because you don't know him, because he abducted you, because he's your enemy. But you find yourself wanting him, regardless of those things. You feel weak, which makes you angry with yourself."

"Yes. That's exactly it."

"Darlin', I understand everything you're feeling right now. I lived it twenty-nine years ago. No one comprehends what you're going through right now more than I do."

"Kieran tells me that I don't have a choice. And that I won't leave this compound without being claimed, by force if need be."

"My situation was very similar. I was barely eighteen when my father told me I was going to marry Nox." That only makes her forty-seven.

"Were you angry?"

"Angry doesn't cover it. I was pissed off, mostly because I fancied myself in love with a boy from The Order. I hated my father. I hated the man he was forcing me to marry. I hated the world and everyone in it. I thought my life was over… and then I met Nox." Her lips form an O and a whistle leaves her mouth. "My God… that man did things to me. Pissed me off. Turned me on. I didn't know if I was coming or going."

Sounds familiar. "How long did you have from the time you met until he claimed you?"

"Three days."

Her situation is more like mine than I thought. "I was under the impression you had more time together."

"I was told about the treaty around a week before Nox came for me. I had a little more time than you to get used to the idea. And I also had my family's encouragement."

"You were claimed… *voluntarily*?"

"I left out the best part." She giggles, making her seem even younger. "Nox spent every minute of our first three days together pursuing me. Romancing me. Winning me over. The man was the master of seduction. By day three, I was ready to jump into bed with him. And that's exactly what I did. Mmm… I enjoyed the hell out of it, too. Often. I was already pregnant with Kieran by the time we married a month later… just as Nox intended."

I'll have the same fate if Kieran has his way.

"You were okay with being pregnant by a man you'd just met?"

"Nox didn't feel like a stranger for long; I quickly came to accept him as my intended. Everything else just fell into place."

"Leaders can't be soft. They must be unmerciful and iron-fisted and hard-hearted. There are times when it's necessary for them to be cruel and savage. How does that work in your marriage?" I only saw it work one way within my parents' marriage. My mother never said a single opposing word to my father.

"Nox is an iron fist inside of a velvet glove. Forceful but soft. Strong yet gentle. It's a delicate balance. He's also everything else I need him to be. Kind. Respectful. Loving. Protective. And Kieran will be all of those things for you as well."

That iron fist part worries me. "I'm not submissive by nature. I have a smart mouth." I grin when I recall what he said about it. "But Kieran says that he likes it."

"He likes a lot of things about you. You're in a very good place, considering the circumstances."

"The biggest difference between your circumstances and mine is that you had your family's support. Your father told you that you were going to marry Lennox. I haven't spoken to my family since I was taken, so it doesn't feel right to accept this fate without a fight."

"I can understand why you feel that way, but becoming Kieran's wife is your fate. It's going to happen with or without your family's support."

"Lennox and Kieran decide everything. They can let me see my family. Or at least let me talk to Thane first."

"Nox and Kieran lead this brotherhood, and they do make all of the decisions, but your fate is the same if you speak to your uncle or not. This was a very well-thought-out plan. It's been decided, and there's no going back."

Arabella can't help me. I'm seeing that now.

"Don't fight this, Westlyn. Don't fight *him*. Willingly give yourself to Kieran. Make it an experience you'll always remember for pleasant reasons. Not dreadful ones."

Arabella speaks fondly about her claiming. It wasn't a horrid experience for her. Maybe it can be enjoyable for me too.

"You've not met Nox?"

"I haven't."

"I think it's time you meet your father-in-law."

Lennox Hendry. The Order leader. *My father-in-law.* That's more than just a little bit intimidating.

Arabella picks up her phone. "Is Kieran with you?" She pauses. "I think so but…" Arabella looks at me and smiles. "I really believe that this transition would go much smoother if she were able to call home first." Another pause. "Don't go anywhere. We're coming to you."

Oh my goodness. I can't believe that she just encouraged Lennox to allow me to call home. "Thank you for doing that."

"Calling home won't change anything, but it could ease your mind going into it. I want to give you that if at all possible."

"Thank you, Ara. I really appreciate it."

"He didn't say yes… but he also didn't say no. We'll see."

Arabella leads me down a hallway and then a staircase to a room located in a basement. Dull. Dark. Dreary. I think it's The Order conference room.

Every man at the table stands when Arabella and I enter. Five pairs of eyes on me. It's unnerving.

I immediately know who Lennox Hendry is based upon appearance alone. Salt and pepper hair. Sable eyes. Tall and broad. An older version of Kieran. "Miss Breckenridge, I'm Lennox. It is a pleasure to meet you."

"Nice to meet you." Not really, but it's the cordial thing to say. And I don't wish to anger him if he's considering letting me call my family. "You have a lovely home."

"It still doesn't feel like home, but I'm sure that will come in time."

"Edinburgh is a wonderful place to live. Have you been able to explore much?"

"Bella and Shaw have done some exploring." He calls his wife Bella. Makes him seem more human.

Arabella's gaze shifts from her husband to me. "We've explored a little, but we'd like to do more. Maybe it'll be safe to do so after the treaty is in effect."

I want to tell Arabella that she and Shaw could explore as much as they like, and The Fellowship wouldn't bother them. Hurting women and children isn't our way. That's been the MO of The Order. Fellowship women are the ones who've been in danger.

"The boys and I have been too occupied with settling brotherhood business to see much of the city." Lennox gestures toward the other men around the table. "These are our other sons, Maddock, Calder, and Carson." Maddock and Calder look like Lennox and Kieran, but Carson is fair and favors Arabella.

We exchange polite banter about it being nice to meet one another, but I don't miss the way each of them is looking at me. Unsettling to have all of these eyes on me at once.

"Boys, your mum and I have a private matter to discuss with Kieran and Westlyn. We'll adjourn for now and pick up with this again tomorrow."

Kieran's brothers file out, but not before one punches him in the arm. "You lucky fucker."

"Tell me about it."

The same brother, I think Maddock, stops in the doorway. "Do any of the other Fellowship women look like you?"

"People say that my sister and I look alike." He doesn't need any ideas about taking Evanna, and I know one sure way to discourage him. "But she's in love with someone. She's already given herself to him."

"Fuck, that's too bad."

There are plenty of attractive single Fellowship women, but I'm not telling him that. This brotherhood doesn't need more motivation for abducting another one of us.

Arabella waits until her other sons are gone. "What do you think, Nox? Would it be okay for Westlyn to call her family? Maybe just for a few minutes?" Lennox sits in his chair and taps his index and middle fingers against the table while looking at me. "I ask on her behalf because after speaking to Westlyn, I believe it would allow things to progress naturally and more smoothly between Kieran and her."

Lennox sighs. "You think it would move the claiming along?"

"I do." Arabella goes to the table and sits beside her husband. She places her hand over his. "I was in her shoes once. You remember how frightened I was? That's multiplied for Westlyn. She was kidnapped by her enemy. She knows none of us, but I'm certain she must think the worst. An encouraging word from her family would go a long way."

"What happens if she calls and the person on the other end orders her to die before submitting?"

"They aren't The Order. The Fellowship is reasonable. No one is going to tell her to do that."

"You don't know that."

"We know how the conversation will go if she calls Isobel," Kieran says.

"Please, Nox. It's what we would want for Shaw if the situation were reversed." Arabella squeezes Lennox's hand. "You're going to deliver our daughter into their hands soon. Please show one of theirs kindness, so the favor will be returned when they have Shaw."

Lennox lifts Arabella's hand and kisses the top. "You're right, Bella. We have to think of Shaw and the way we want her to be treated after she goes to them." He looks at me. "You may speak to Isobel, but in front of us and on speaker. We can't give you privacy."

"Thank you."

Kieran takes my phone from his jacket pocket and holds it out. I can't believe it's been within my reach all this time. Not that it would have done me much good if I'd gotten my hands on it. "Thank you."

I'm not at all surprised when Isobel answers on the first ring. "Wes?"

"It's me."

"Oh, darlin', I knew ye were safe, but I'm still relieved to hear yer voice. Can ye tell me what's happening?"

I want to verify Kieran's story and see if he really spoke with Isobel or if he was lying to persuade my decision. "Kieran told me that he and his father spoke with you last night?"

"We spoke briefly."

Okay. He was telling the truth about that much. "And you know about the marriage treaty? That they want me to marry Lennox and Arabella's oldest son?"

"I'm aware, and I fully support yer union to him. I'm well acquainted with Lennox, and I trust him. Yer marriage tae his son will bring an end tae the war between oor brotherhoods."

I can't look at Kieran when I say the next part. "He's planning to claim me and I…"

"What is it?"

"It feels wrong to give him my consent without talking to the family since our marriage involves the future of both brotherhoods."

"Thane has decided that he is going tae agree tae the marriage treaty. One of ye will marry Kieran Hendry, and either Jamie or Mitch will marry their daughter."

There's my answer. No more reason to wrestle with indecision or uncertainty. I'm going to give myself to Kieran of my own free will. "Tell everyone to not worry about me. Everything's going to be okay."

"Yes, it is. But I need ye tae keep this conversation a secret between us. And also the one I had with Lennox and Kieran last night. Thane would be furious if he knew I interfered."

"You don't have to say any more. I understand completely." Women are viewed as incapable when it comes to Fellowship business. Dumbest shite I ever heard of. But I'm not sure that's the case here among the Hendrys. Looks to me like Lennox listens to Arabella.

"Will you pass the phone to Lennox?"

"Yes. I love you."

"I love ye too."

Kieran and me. We are going to happen and soon, judging by the predatory look in Kieran's eyes.

He comes to me, takes my hand in his, and tugs me toward the door. "Come."

This is it. Once this deed is done, it can't be undone.

I'm his forever.

CHAPTER NINE

KIERAN HENDRY

I GRASP Westlyn's hips after we're inside my quarters and push her backward until she's pinned against the back of the door. I move close, so close that we're chest-to-chest. The tip of her tongue peeks out when she licks her lips, and I briefly press my mouth to hers before sucking her bottom lip into my mouth. Our kiss turns into a game of biting and nipping and sucking. Until it's no longer playful and our kiss becomes fiery and intense and demanding.

I break our kiss. "Are you freely giving yourself to me?"

Westlyn nods, but it's not enough to satisfy me. I want the words to come from her mouth. "I need to hear you say it." She grins and looks down—something else I'm not having. I place my hand under her chin, lifting her face to make our eyes connect. "Look at me when you say the words."

"I am freely giving myself to you."

I find her hand and bring it up, turning it so the engagement ring is on display. "And your answer to my proposal?"

"Ask me again."

"Will you be my wife?"

She smiles. "Yes… I will be your wife."

I press a kiss to the ring on her hand. "You're mine from this moment on. No other man will touch you. Ever."

"Is the same true for you? No other woman will touch you? Ever?"

I don't mistake the challenge in her voice. Westlyn isn't familiar with The Syndicate or our ways. I think it's time to educate her. "I don't know how it's done in The Fellowship, but we are faithful to our partners. When I claim you, you also claim me. Just as you owe me your faithfulness and loyalty and devotion, I owe you the same. I have had many women before you, but there will be no more. I will never stray from you."

Her arms wrapping around my neck and her lips landing upon mine are simultaneous. I didn't know that she'd get so turned on by hearing me promise to always be faithful. I'd have already done so had I known.

I grasp her hips and use my grip to tug her toward the bed, kissing en route. I'm dissatisfied with the slow pace, so I grasp the back of her thighs and lift her, wrapping her legs around my waist.

She tightens her hold around my neck, and it doesn't lessen even when we reach the bed. Together, we fall on the mattress with me on top, my body a perfect fit between her legs. My mouth moves down the side of her neck and I kiss and suck her skin... hard. Marking her. I want her to wear the evidence of my claiming for all to see. Every man who looks at her will know that she's been taken.

Her body tenses, and her breath quickens when my hand slides under her sweater and dips into her bra. I roll her nipple between my thumb and index finger, and it instantly hardens.

Nervous little virgin. It's going to be so much fun making her come. But first I need to get her used to the feel of our bodies coming together.

I bend her knee and bring her leg up so it's wrapped around my waist, our bodies fitting together perfectly. Then I rock my hard cock against her pussy, and it only takes a few thrusts before she's moving with me.

I gather her sweater in my hand and push it upward. Moving lower, I nibble the skin on her stomach and waist. I fucking love it when she pants and squirms beneath me, so I push down the waistband of her pants and kiss and lick the skin on her lower belly to see what kind of reaction I can get. I'm pleased when her body jerks and jolts when I move lower. Fuck, she's going to detonate like an atomic bomb when I go down on her.

I push her sweater higher. "Let's get this off of you."

She lifts her head and shoulders from the bed and I pull her top up and over her head. Her breasts are thrust upward in a black and white lace push-up bra. Sexy as fuck. I palm both, gently squeezing and releasing them, before I reach behind her and unclasp her bra. Prettiest pair of tits I've ever seen. So full. So plump. So rosy pink. I can't resist cupping one from the bottom and lowering my mouth to lick the bud before sucking her whole nipple into my mouth.

My suit is restricting my movement so I rise to a kneeling position and remove my jacket, tossing it at the bench at the foot of my bed. I pull the knot of my tie until the loop is large enough to slip it over my head. I'm surprised when Westlyn sits up, untucks my shirt, and goes to work on unbuttoning it. And it turns me the fuck on. But my dick turns to steel when she tugs open the button on my pants and lowers the zipper.

I slide off the side of the bed and watch Westlyn work on removing her pants while I rid myself of my remaining clothes. She's down to only her black and white lace knickers. I'm glad she leaves them on. I want to be the one to slide them down her legs.

I crawl onto the bed on all fours and hook my fingers into the skinny black elastic straps over her hips. She lifts her bum and I drag the knickers down her legs. I fist the black fabric, and Westlyn's eyes widen when I bring it to my nose and inhale deeply. Fuck, the scent of her pussy is delicious.

I crawl over Westlyn and lower my body so that I'm lying on top of her, bare skin against bare skin. My mouth comes down on hers gently. Our kiss is soft and slow and sultry. I can't recall ever kissing this way. Can't remember ever wanting a woman this much.

My mouth leaves hers and moves lower. Down her neck. Down her chest. Down her stomach. "I'm about to make you feel so good. A good like you've never known."

Westlyn lifts her head and looks down at me hovering over her stomach. "What are you going to do?"

"I'm going to make you come. Hard." I'm going to make it so good that one time won't ever be enough to satisfy her.

CHAPTER TEN
WESTLYN BRECKENRIDGE

I'M GOING to make you come. Hard.

I'm still looking down at Kieran, his eyes on mine, when his tongue darts out and he licks the top of my slit peeking out above the Y where my legs meet. Ho… ly… shite. The tingles spinning in my lower pelvis are out of control and I realize that my mouth is gaping open when I hear my own breathing. No, not breathing. Panting.

Kieran moves lower and pushes my legs back and apart. His wet tongue swipes up my center slowly. Softly. "Oh my God."

"Feels good?"

"Yesss."

"Then you're really going to like this."

He spreads my slit apart with his fingers and his tongue does this fast vibration-flicking thing that taps against the sensitive nub at the top. "Ohhh… ohh… ohh."

I reach overhead and grasp the edge of the bed when he inserts his finger, or fingers. They thrust in and out, rubbing something inside me. What, I'm not sure, but it feels so damn good. I can't stop my body from rocking against his face and hand.

"Ohh… oh… Kieran… I think I'm… coming." He sucks harder, and my body jolts with a contraction low in my pelvis. A rhythmic squeeze-and-release pleasure explodes inside me, and a warm rush fills my face and chest and arms and legs. I get so wet that it feels like it's trickling. My legs tense, my toes curl. Tingly warmth floods my face, neck, hands, and feet as I ride this pleasure to the fullest extent.

Ecstasy. Elation. Euphoria.

Kieran wasn't lying. He made me come hard.

My body is completely lax except for my trembling legs when Kieran crawls over me and lowers his naked body on top of mine. We're face-to-face, heart-to-heart, and skin-on-skin when he presses a soft kiss to my mouth. "Did you enjoy me eating your pussy?" His vulgar mouth is just the icing on top of my cake.

"I enjoyed it very much. I hope it's something you'll do again."

"No worries, doll. I love the taste of your pussy. I'm going to eat it often." Such a filthy thing to say. And hot.

Kieran nestles between my legs and rotates his hips, rubbing the length of his erection against me. This is it. He's about to claim me. "I'm not on birth control."

"Good." Kieran reaches between our bodies and positions the tip of his cock at my entrance. "Where are you in your cycle?"

"I think it's been around two weeks since I had my period." Maybe. Not really sure since I've not had a reason to keep up with it.

"You could be ovulating."

"I guess so."

"I hope so. I want to put our firstborn inside you as soon as possible."

Shite. A baby is no joke. A baby joins me to him forever. A baby makes all of this very surreal.

I am going to be the wife of a leader. It is our duty to seal this union as soon as possible and produce the next generation of leaders. This isn't news to me, but it's still frightening, and so is what comes next. Kieran's cock is going to stretch my body. Rip my virginity. Cause me pain. But then it's going to bring me pleasure. My desire for pleasure outweighs my fear of pain.

I crave Kieran. I want everything he plans to do to me. I'm ready for this.

Kieran inserts the head, and I dig my fingertips into the flesh on his back when he pushes his cock inside me. I bury my face against the bend between his neck and shoulder, but my gasp is still loud. I believe the worst is over, but I find out that I'm wrong when he pushes the remaining length inside me, ripping through the last of my innocence.

Fuck. That. Hurt.

And now it's done. There's no going back. My virginity belongs to Kieran Hendry, and so do I. A man I don't love, but I'm still his forever.

He's unmoving, his cock deep inside me, and he raises his head to look at me. "Did that hurt badly?"

The person I am inside is screaming that I can't show him weakness. "No."

"Don't lie to me, Westlyn."

He knows that I'm a virgin and that he has a huge dick. Denying the pain is an obvious lie. "It hurt a lot, but it's subsiding."

"I'm going to start moving, slowly, but tell me if it hurts." He pulls back and slowly thrusts inside me again, watching my face. He smiles, I guess pleased with the expression he sees. "You're good?"

I nod. "I'm okay."

Kieran's pace increases, and I tilt my hips upward with each of his thrusts. He pulls back, almost to the point where it feels like he's going to slide out, and then quickly thrusts back in. He grasps the backs of my thighs and pushes my legs up and apart, using them as leverage to pound into me deeper and harder. "I can't believe how fucking good you feel. It's so much different."

Does that mean that I feel better than the women he's had before me?

He releases my legs and lowers his body, his chest pressing against my breasts. His forearms are pushing into the mattress around my head, trapping me inside his cage of muscular arms. His mouth covers mine, and they become one, just as our bodies.

Kieran's hand finds mine, and he brings my palm to his chest. He spreads it over his heart and then does the same with his hand over my chest. "Mo chroí. Say it with me to complete the claiming."

A Fellowship brother says, 'into me, you see' when he claims a woman. I'm not sure what I expected people from The Syndicate or The Order to say to one another but I never expected 'mo chroí.' It's Gaelic, meaning *my heart*. Saying that to someone is very intimate and special. It's not something to be taken lightly... and damn if I don't love it.

I press my hand to his heart, and I think his is beating even harder and faster than mine. "Mo chroí," we say together.

We're doing this for the future of our people, but the smile on his face isn't duty. The gentleness he's showing me isn't duty. The intimacy we're sharing isn't duty.

He presses his forehead to mine, and his breath increases. A groan accompanies the last few thrusts. "Uhhh…oooh… fuck, I'm coming… so hard." Filling me with his seed.

He stills and lifts his face so that we can make eye contact. I wait to see what he'll say, but nothing comes. Instead, he kisses my mouth, pulls out slowly, and rolls away to lie beside me.

He lies there panting for a moment until he catches his breath. "That was so fucking good."

I've seen movies and read books and heard all kinds of things from my girls, but all of that went out the window when he got on top of me. "I wasn't sure what I should do."

"I love that you didn't know what to do. Our first time should only be about me taking you. Making you mine. It was perfect." He lifts my hand to his mouth and places a kiss on top. "And now you are mine. Forever."

"I am."

I think this is the time when true lovers would talk about how much they love each other, but that's not going to happen between us. Our relationship, if it can even be called that, is the epitome of putting the cart before the horse. "I don't know you at all."

"What would you like to know?"

I guess we should go back to the beginning. "Tell me about growing up in The Syndicate."

"My grandfather, Douglas Hendry, is leader of The Syndicate. My father's older brother, William, will become leader when my grandfather passes, which will probably be soon because he isn't well."

"I'm sorry to hear that."

"Grandfather has had a long run. He's tired and ready to go. My uncle will be a good leader. He's been trained for it since he was a boy."

"Does your uncle have sons?"

"Two. My father was never going to have a chance at being leader. As the second son, he accepted that a long time ago, and he was content to sit on the council."

"But he was still trained as though he might one day lead?" It's the way. Just as Jamie has been trained, to some degree, to lead.

"Aye, as was I." He shakes his head as though he's still in disbelief. "I never thought I'd be at the top of the hierarchy, and now here I am, the next leader of The Order. And you are going to be the wife of a leader, just not the one you thought."

"I never thought I was going to marry Sin." The whole notion was just ridiculous.

"Then what did you see in your future?"

"I was planning to leave The Fellowship. Marry someone normal."

"Well, half of that actually happened. You've left The Fellowship."

"True." I giggle and feel a gush of something wet and sticky between my legs. I don't want Kieran to think that I'm gross. "I feel dirty down there. I should clean up."

"Just semen and virginal blood. It's to be expected." Kieran catches my wrist when I try to sit up. "Not yet, just in case you're ovulating."

He isn't kidding around about trying to conceive. "You heard what Isobel said. Thane is agreeing to the treaty. I don't have to get pregnant right away."

"I heard what she said, and I also know that I'm not taking chances. A bairn is the only way to ensure that our bond can't be undone."

I want more of this. Lying in bed talking, learning what kind of man Kieran Hendry really is. "I'd like to get to know my husband before a baby comes into the picture."

"No worries. You'll have plenty of time to get to know me before our baby comes."

Kieran rises and moves to kneel between my legs. He pushes them apart and cups his hands over my mound. He glides his fingers up and down my sticky, wet center. His fingertip grazes my clit with every upward stroke, enough to stimulate but not nearly enough to satisfy. It's torture, the sweetest kind. "I have a plan for how I'll keep you occupied while you lie here and wait. You're going to like this."

He wasn't wrong the last time he said that. He places his fingers over the top of my slit and rubs it in a circular motion. My entire groin throbs. Every nerve ending between my legs is alive.

I tilt my hips and rock against his hand while he works my clit. I lift my arms over my head and grasp the pillow under my head. "Kieran… please don't stop doing that."

"I fucking love hearing you say my name while you're writhing in pleasure."

I tense all over when the rhythmic contractions in my groin begin. Once. Twice. I lose count of how many times my body contracts and clenches. "Oh my God. I'm coming *again*."

I relax when it ends, and my entire body goes slack. That includes allowing my thighs to fall completely apart. I feel another wet ooze, but I don't have it in me to care if Kieran sees the bloody mess between my legs. And I don't think he minds anyway. He was more than happy to cause it.

"That was beautiful to watch."

"That was beautiful to experience."

Kieran lies down beside me and flattens his palm against my stomach. "I'm relieved that you're not prudish." He slowly moves it upward and palms the underside of my breast. The act feels more exploratory than sexual. "I think we're going to have a very healthy sex life."

"I hope so." I've seen how important sex is in a healthy relationship through Bleu, Ellison, and Evanna. I've also seen the flip side where bad decisions regarding sex can drive apart two people who love one another. Leith and Lorna belong together. Everyone seems to know that except them.

I place my hand on top of his. "Our relationship is off to a good start. It would be off to a better one if you'd let me see Ellison."

"No."

"It's a hard no without any kind of discussion about it?"

"Correct."

"Kieran... I've given you my virginity. I've agreed to be your wife. I let you come inside me, and now I'm lying here to increase the odds of conceiving. I'm in this with you. What more could I do at this point to convince you?"

"You are in this with me, and I don't need your friend trying to persuade you otherwise."

"I've bent for you. A lot. Surely, you can bend for me, just a little." I'm not asking for that much. "I know Ellison must be losing her mind with worry. She has no idea if Jamie is dead or alive. And she's probably fearing the worst for me. I'd like to put an end to her anxiety." I see the indecision behind his eyes. "You could go with me. Stand at the door and listen while I speak to her."

He sighs. "I don't know."

"You said that you wanted to please your wife. Seeing Ellison would please me."

"That's not what I meant."

"You're still treating me like your captive. Not like the woman you're going to marry soon."

He groans beneath his breath, reminding me of some kind of beast. "I'll give you two minutes with her."

I roll and climb on top of Kieran, straddling him, and press a kiss to his mouth. "Thank you."

He smacks my bum. "You're supposed to be on your back letting my swimmers do their thing."

I grin. "Then I guess we'll have to do it all over again."

I OPEN the door and Ellison is lying on the bed in the dark. She lifts her head and squints when the light from the hallway hits her face. "Wes!" She leaps from the bed, and we meet in the middle of the room. "Please tell me that you're all right."

"Two minutes, Westlyn."

Ellison grabs my hands and pulls me to sit on the bed beside her. I can see that she's straining to see my face since the only light in the room is coming from the doorway. "I'm so sorry. I know the last two days have been hell for you. Has he beaten you horribly?"

I can't tell Ellison about the marriage treaty. At least not yet. I don't have time to explain everything that has happened, and I can't have her in here freaking out about it. And that's exactly what she'd do.

I squeeze her hands. "I'm okay."

"How can you be okay?" I hear the disbelief in her voice, and I understand it completely after the threats Kieran made the night he kidnapped us.

"Don't fret about me. I'm all right. Really." I know Ellison must think

I'm putting on a strong front, but surely she can see that I've not been abused.

"Have you heard anything about Jamie?"

"Kieran told me that he's alive."

Ellison looks up toward the ceiling. "Oh, thank God." She takes the few seconds she needs to absorb the good news and then leans closer and whispers, "What is going to happen to us?"

I want to ease my friend's worries without alarming her about what has happened. "Kieran left me in his quarters right after we arrived. I think he and the new Order council went to meet with Thane, Sin, Mitch, and Jamie. That's all I know, but I get the feeling they must have negotiated for our return."

"When?"

Kieran didn't tell me how long he was planning to keep us before he and the council return to discuss the treaty. "I have no idea. Guess it depends on the terms of the negotiation."

"Time's up, Westlyn. Back to my quarters."

"Is that where you've been confined all of this time? His quarters?"

I was, but I'm not exactly confined now. Can't tell her that. "Yes."

"I'm so sorry that you're going through this ordeal."

I need her to see that I'm all right so she doesn't continue to worry. "Look at me, and listen to what I'm telling you, Ellison. Really hear my words. It's. Okay."

"How can it be?" She doesn't understand now, but she will soon.

"Westlyn… you're done here."

"I have to go. Stay strong. Everything is going to be fine."

We embrace one another, and she whispers, "You stay strong."

I wish I could tell Ellison the whole story so that she can comprehend that I'm truly all right. But that'll come later when I have time to explain everything.

CHAPTER ELEVEN

KIERAN HENDRY

WESTLYN DIDN'T TELL Ellison that I'd claimed her or that we were going to be married. I thought she'd be eager to share the news with one of her best friends. "You didn't say anything about us."

"You gave me two minutes with her. I couldn't throw that kind of information at her when I didn't have time to explain the situation from start to end. In case you've forgotten, she isn't Fellowship. She wouldn't understand anything about our marriage treaty. There was no way to make her comprehend in a matter of a couple of minutes why I'd agree to something like that. She'd have been even more worried instead of less."

"I guess."

"You could have given me more time with her, especially if you wanted me to talk about us and everything that has happened."

"You're angry with me." I hear it in her clipped tone.

"I'm annoyed."

I love that she feels like she can be honest and tell me such things. People are typically afraid of saying something to offend me.

"Two minutes wasn't enough time to say much of anything."

"Try to understand my position. I couldn't risk your friend convincing you that marrying me is a mistake."

"It wouldn't matter if she successfully convinced me or not. What's done between us is done, and it can't be taken back. I'm yours, Kieran."

I love hearing her say that she's mine. "Yes, you are." I pull her into my arms and press a kiss to her lips. "Would you like to shower before bed?"

"I would love a shower."

I thought so. She didn't seem to be much of a fan of postcoital body fluids. But it's something that she'll need to get used to. There's going to be a lot of that swapped between us.

"Is it okay if I join you? I could use a shower myself."

She nibbles her bottom lip and nods. "Mmm-hmm."

"Would you like Nan to change the sheets while we bathe?"

Westlyn's cute little nose scrunches. "I hate for her to have to do that, but I don't want to sleep on bloodstained sheets tonight."

"She won't mind." I kiss the top of her head. "Go start the shower and I'll be there after I call Nan."

Westlyn is massaging a thick white lather into her hair when I enter the shower. "I was planning to do that for you."

"Do what?"

"Shampoo your hair."

"You want to wash my hair?"

"Aye. I've never done it before. And I'd like to do that for you." Seems like something special you'd do for your wife.

"Okay, if you want." She turns so that she's facing away from me. "Have at it."

I squeeze additional shampoo into my palm and massage it into her hair, creating a huge ball of white lather. I don't have much in the fingernail department since I keep them trimmed short, but I use what I have to scratch her scalp. "Does that feel good?"

"Hmm… mmm."

"I love your hair. The color. How long it is. The way you wear it. How soft it feels compared to mine."

"Yours is very different from mine." She turns around and reaches for the top of my head. "Aye, that is some thick, coarse hair you have there, sir. I don't think you'll ever go bald."

"Yours is like silk. Very feminine."

"I was surprised when I saw your mother's fair hair and eyes."

Most people are. We're total opposites, but I think my eyes are shaped like hers. "Wait until you see my sister. She looks like Daenerys Targaryen."

"Her hair is lighter than your mother's?"

Hair so blond, it's almost white. "Yes. And her eyes are an even paler blue."

"Why haven't I met your sister?"

I'm ashamed of Shaw's behavior right now. No Hendry should be acting the way she is. "Shaw is pissed off at the world right now. She's lashing out like a child."

"How old is she?"

"Eighteen."

"Eighteen is a child. And for the record, I'd probably have done the same if I'd been told five years ago that I was going to be handed over to another brotherhood to marry a man I'd never met. Perhaps you shouldn't be so hard on her?"

It's true. I've been stern with her, probably more so than I needed to be, but it's because I don't want Westlyn to think poorly of her. "I've forbidden Shaw from having contact with you until she pulls herself together. I don't want you to meet her while she's behaving badly. She's a sweet lass. Just young and strong-willed."

"I don't dislike strong-willed. I'm a little bit that way myself."

"Yes, you are. You and Shaw are a lot alike in that way. You're alike in a lot of ways, actually."

"I look forward to meeting her."

"I hope that she accepts her fate soon. I'm sure Thane will expect us to deliver her into Mitch's care as soon as the final agreement is made. It'll complicate things if Jamie or Mitch refuses to marry her because of her behavior." And I don't like complications.

"Jamie loves Ellison. He isn't going to marry Shaw. And I don't think you really want your sister to be married to a man who loves another woman. Mitch is unattached. She should marry him."

Mitch is the second son of the leader. "His position is more ideal than your brother's."

"Jamie will never have a chance at being leader. He knows that and doesn't care. He would much rather be a doctor. Mitch will one day be second-in-command. He would be the better choice if you want Shaw to be married to someone who takes leadership seriously."

"We'd prefer that."

"My father was second-in-command. It isn't a bad place to be."

"You know what else isn't a bad place to be?"

"Tell me."

"In this shower with you." I wrap my arms around Westlyn from behind and glide my hands over her wet skin to palm her breasts and kiss the side of her neck. "Your hair isn't the only thing I'm fond of."

She leans against me, pressing her wet back against my front, and covers my hands with hers. "What else are you fond of?"

"I have a deep appreciation for these." I move my hand from one breast to cup her between her legs, gliding my middle finger into the center of her split and finding that hardened nub. "And I love this."

The pace of her breathing increases when I push my finger back and forth, flicking her clit.

"You are so good at that."

"Come for me again." Tonight is all about Westlyn and her pleasure. Laying the groundwork for the intimate relationship I want to have with her from this night forward. Turning my intended into a willing, wanting, always-ready-for-sex vixen.

I introduce another finger and change to a twitchy, side-to-side motion. "Is that good?"

Her hips buck against my hand. "Oh God."

"I take that as a yes."

"Yes, fuck, yes." More bucking. Squirming. Writhing. "I'm coming."

"Boss…"

No fucking way. No fucking way a brother is brave enough to enter my quarters without permission. No fucking way a brother is standing at the entrance to my bathroom while I'm in the shower with Westlyn. Standing there like some kind of dumb fucker while I rub her off.

I cover Westlyn's mouth with my free hand and smother her moans. We twist and I shield her naked body with mine so she can't be seen by this dumb asshole. "Get the fuck out of here. Now!"

"My apologies, boss. You didn't answer your phone." The man's voice is trembling.

"Because I'm in the fucking shower." With my mate.

"Your father sent for you. Says it's an emergency."

My father knows I'm with Westlyn. Claiming her. Sealing our bond. Locking in our future with The Fellowship. He knows how pivotal this moment is. He wouldn't have sent for me unless it's urgent. Again.

"Where is my father?"

"The conference room."

"Tell him that I'll be right there."

"Yes, sir."

Westlyn turns in my arms, and I grasp the sides of her face. "We'll pick up with this when I return."

"I don't know what has happened, but I assume it's not good. If you have to go out… *to solve a problem*, please be careful."

Her plea sounds like that of a true mate. "I'm always careful, doll." I place a quick kiss against her mouth and step out of the shower, not even taking time to dry off before putting the same clothes back on.

I'm adjusting my tie when I enter the conference room. A leader can never be seen appearing less than professional.

"I was beginning to wonder if you were going to be able to stop fucking your new mate long enough to join us," Maddock says. "I bet it was difficult to tear yourself away from that pussy."

My brother always likes to see how far he can push me. I give him plenty of leeway, but that's over when it comes to Westlyn. "Because you're my brother, I'm going to allow you that one transgression against my mate. But heed my warning: never say my mate's name and the word pussy in the same sentence again, or you'll be sorry."

"Damn. My brother is ready to defend the honor of a woman? Her pussy must be pure magic." He grins. "I didn't say her name."

I warned him, and yet he's continuing to push me where Westlyn is concerned. I can't let that go.

I charge across the room and grab Maddock around the throat, pulling him from his chair, and shoving him against the wall. "I told you to not address my mate in that manner."

"Shite, Kieran. Maddock was just fucking around," Calder says. "You're choking him."

"I'm not fucking around with you." There's a growl to my voice. "Not when it comes to her."

"Calm the fuck down," Calder says. He places his hand on my shoulder. "He was kidding."

I release my hold on Maddock's throat and shove him toward his seat. "Do not disrespect my mate again, even in jest."

My brother reaches for the front of his throat. "You're out of your fucking mind over that woman."

"Kieran is taking his role as her mate seriously, just as he should. That makes me very proud."

I straighten my suit, and then Maddock and I join our father and other brothers at the table. I immediately know something bad has gone down when I see the expression on my father's face. "We have another fucking problem."

"Another?" Carson says.

"Your brother and I had to handle a situation this morning involving several Order members."

"And golden boy has ensured that they'll no longer be a problem?"

My brothers are jealous of the dependency our father has on my skills. It's true. I am a huge asset to our brotherhood, but they don't understand the burden that goes along with it. They only see the glory and praise. Never the pain and suffering.

"Kieran fixed that problem and now twelve hours later, we have another. Two dead Order women were dumped on our own doorstep thirty minutes ago. The women were nineteen and twenty-one years old. Sisters. Their father is devastated and demanding blood. Fellowship blood."

I feel inclined to defend Westlyn's brotherhood. "Of course, their father deserves justice, but not against The Fellowship. They didn't do this. They don't attack women."

"Agreed. Harming women is the MO of The Order." I'm relieved to hear my father say that.

"Are you saying that brothers from The Order killed two of their own women to frame The Fellowship?" Maddock's voice is raw and hoarse. Perhaps I choked him a little too hard.

"That's exactly what I'm saying."

"They hate The Fellowship badly enough to do something that despicable?" Carson is the youngest and hasn't been around brotherhood issues as much. He sometimes fails to understand all the evil that goes along with it.

"Absolutely."

"How do we prove it?"

"The four men who brought the dead sisters to our doorstep are dumb fucks. They didn't even cover their faces. I have them on video." My father holds up a remote, and a video begins playing on the large flat-screen. "I don't know who they are, but one is marked." He zooms in on the neck of one of the men. "There… behind his ear. He wears the symbol of The Order."

"Someone will know who they are."

"I think it's time we hold another meeting with our new people, all of them, to demonstrate what happens when someone commits treason. I'm going to put out the word that we are having a party tomorrow night. Every member of The Order must be in attendance. When it's over, everyone is going to have a full understanding of the way things are going to be from now on. They won't dare to cross us again."

"There are many Order members working inside the compound. I'm concerned one of them might try to harm Westlyn. I think it's wise to keep her by my side until this is handled."

"I know it goes against our plan, and you're not going to like it, but I think Westlyn needs to return to The Fellowship until we tend to our affairs within The Order."

No fucking way. "She is my mate. Mine to protect. She will stay by my side." No other way makes sense. "I did not claim her only to return her to The Fellowship."

"Westlyn is yours to protect, and that's exactly what you'll be doing by sending her back to her people for safekeeping until this problem is rectified." My father hesitates. "You'll be apart for no more than a few days."

"I'll appear weak in their eyes if I send her back for the purpose of protection."

"No, son. They'll see you for the strong leader you are. The leader who does what is necessary to protect your mate even when that means admitting that the safest place for her may be somewhere other than next to you." That's not how this feels. "This would be a different situation if we were dealing with The Syndicate. We'd have security we trusted, but this is The Order and your mate is Fellowship. She's hated. And she may not be safe here until we use our iron fist to take control of this brotherhood."

"What if The Fellowship won't let me have Westlyn back? What then?"

"That isn't going to happen. You've had her."

Damn right, I've had her. And I'm not done having her.

"It's possible you've already sealed your bond. They won't refuse to return your claimed mate to you."

"I won't give her up. If I have to perch on top of Thane's house and snipe every Fellowship brother down, I will."

"I trust that it won't come down to that."

Westlyn Breckenridge is mine.

I will go to fucking war with The Order, The Fellowship, or whoever for her if I must.

CHAPTER TWELVE
WESTLYN BRECKENRIDGE

I STAND in the closet and look through the pieces of lingerie hanging there. Another ivory silk gown. A black one. A red. A floral. Some of it is downright naughty. And I'm excited about wearing it... but after I've had more time with Kieran. I'm not brave enough to go there just yet.

I'm slipping into the black silk gown, no panties, when there's a knock at the door. "Who is it?"

"Kieran's sister."

He told me that she isn't supposed to have contact with me until her behavior changes. I somehow think showing up at the door while Kieran is gone isn't a good indicator that has happened.

I put on the gown's matching robe. "Hurry up and let me in."

I open the door and a streak of white-blond hair darts into Kieran's suite. Shaw Hendry is the complete opposite of Kieran in every way. Tiny. Fair. Delicate. She's easily one of the most unique beauties I've ever seen. "Are you Westlyn Breckenridge? From The Fellowship?"

"I am."

"Thank God I was able to get to you while the council is meeting. I'm Shaw, and it's lovely to meet you. I'm sorry to ambush you this way, but my brother is being a total asshole about introducing us."

This isn't what Kieran ordered. His sister is blatantly going against his orders, and I'm afraid that's going to cause a problem. "It's nice to meet you too, but I don't want Kieran to be angry because you're here."

"Oh, fuck Kieran." I think I recall saying something very similar not so long ago. "I'm here because I need to talk to you."

She crosses her arms. "In case you don't know, I'm the other half of the marriage treaty. I'm being forced to marry a Breckenridge."

"Kieran told me, and he says that you aren't happy about it."

"Fuck no, I'm not happy. I'm mad as hell. Aren't you?"

"I was."

She looks bewildered by my answer. "How can you not still be pissed off?"

"Our circumstances are different. I had no prospects for a husband from within my brotherhood. I never had the intention to marry a Fellowship man. Of course, I wasn't happy about being kidnapped and threatened and told who I was going to marry, but it turns out that I think Kieran and I are compatible."

"I've been raising hell for a week, but I don't think I'm going to get out of marrying Jamie or Mitch."

I hope she doesn't prefer Jamie over Mitch. "You won't marry my brother. Jamie is already in love with someone. He will not give her up even for the good of the brotherhood."

"Then that leaves me with Mitch. I need to know everything about him. Good or bad, I want to hear it all. Because I'm losing my mind thinking about marrying a man whom I've never met."

Kieran says that Shaw has been irrational, but I see only a scared girl. "Mitch is kind and considerate and respectful. He's slow to anger, but once he gets there, you better look out because he's a beast. He may be the second-born son, but he is strong and loyal and dutiful to the brotherhood."

"How old is he?"

"Just turned twenty-four."

"Is he hideous-looking? Please don't lie or sugarcoat it."

I can't control my laughter. "No. Mitch is a handsome man. Tall, muscular, fit. Dark hair. Deep brown eyes, but not nearly as dark as Kieran's. Mitch's are a rich shade of brown, like warm chocolate. All of the Fellowship women think he's very good-looking. They'd all love to be claimed by him, but he's never found one to interest him."

"He's not gay?"

"No. Mitch is definitely not gay."

"I don't think I'd mind him being gay. At least then he wouldn't want to have sex with me." She frowns and shakes her head. "I just can't imagine doing it for the first time, or any time, with a man I don't know."

"It sounds crazy, and I don't know how to explain it, but being intimate with Kieran doesn't feel like being with a stranger."

"I don't understand how that's possible. He is a stranger. You've just met."

"We have this crazy, intense sexual chemistry. It's out of this world. I guess it fuels the relationship." I'm not sure what will happen between us after it plateaus.

"Don't be fooled by my brother. He can be sweet when he wants to be, but he's an asshole when it comes to women." She doesn't know the half of it. "They fall all over him like he's some kind of king, and he doesn't care whose heart he breaks as long as he gets what he wants."

"Your brother has already clearly demonstrated what an asshole he can be. And I showed him what a bitch I can be, but we've talked and come to an understanding."

"What kind of understanding?"

"If we must be married for the good of our brotherhoods, we're going to make the best of it. Our marriage is going to be real."

"Kieran has already claimed you?"

"Yes."

"You were a virgin?"

"I was."

"Was it horrible?" This poor girl looks terrified.

"No. I liked it." I can't stop my grin from spreading. "I liked it a lot."

"I hate asking because it was with my brother, but what was it like?"

"Have your friends not told you about being claimed?"

"None of my friends have been claimed, and I'm not allowed to associate with girls who would allow men to bed them. My parents have sheltered me."

Wow. This girl really has been guarded by Lennox and Arabella.

"I know the feeling all too well. My father threatened every brother within The Fellowship with severe mangling or death if they so much as looked my way."

"Same. The men of The Syndicate acted as though I didn't exist. I don't know if it's because they found me revolting or because they feared the wrath of my father and brothers."

The only daughter with four very large older brothers. I can see where that would be intimidating for a boy who was interested in Shaw.

"You're a beautiful girl. Surely you must know that no man could possibly find you revolting."

She shrugs. "I have no way of really knowing when they avoid me like the plague."

"I can promise you that Mitch will not find you revolting. He'll think you are the most beautiful girl he's ever seen." They'll make a very cute couple.

"You haven't told me what the claiming was like. Please... I need someone besides my mother to tell me what's going to happen."

It's awkward telling my young sister-in-law about being claimed. And it's more awkward to tell her that I was really into it because her brother made me so horny. Definitely need to tone that part down. "Kieran wanted to make it good for me. He went slow and was gentle. I won't lie to you. It still hurt... but not for long. A minute at most. The pleasure made me forget about the brief moment of pain."

"I know his duty was to seal your bond. Do you think he did?"

"Maybe. I'm not sure about the timing because I haven't been keeping up with my cycles." If it didn't happen, I suspect it will soon.

"It'll be Mitch's duty to seal our bond as soon as possible, but I don't want to have a baby right now. Do you?"

"I'd prefer to wait, but I'm okay with it if it happens." Actually, after being around Sin and Bleu's babies, I might be more than okay with it.

"I'm not okay with it. Not even a little."

"Your feelings might change if things go well between you and Mitch."

"Do you really think things could go well between us?"

"If you'd asked me before tonight, I'd have said no. But after being claimed by Kieran, I know it could go very well."

Shaw is younger, but her circumstances are different than mine. Better in a lot of ways. She's been told by her family what's going to happen. She'll be delivered to Mitch, not stolen by him. Or threatened. Her family is encouraging this union. Her marriage to Mitch has real potential. "If anyone understands your uneasiness, it's me. I truly believe that you could be happy with Mitch. Especially if you're inclined to make it work, even a small bit."

The door opens, and Kieran stills when he sees Shaw. "What the fuck are you doing in here?" His voice is a roar. A growl. So loud it's nearly deafening. "I ordered you to not have contact with Westlyn until I said it was permitted."

Shaw stands in place, saying nothing. I think terrified. Or pissed off. I can't decide which, but I feel the need to shield her from Kieran's wrath. "Don't be angry. She just wanted to meet her new sister-in-law."

"It's okay. You don't have to protect me from this asshole."

"Watch your mouth, Shaw. Despite what you may think, you're not too big or old for me to belt."

"You're not my father."

"And you'd better be damn glad of that because I wouldn't overlook your bullshit as he does."

Shaw bats her lashes and grins. "I have Dad wrapped around my little finger, don't I?"

"Not for much longer. Your arse is getting carted off to The Fellowship in four days."

"In four days?" The color leaves Shaw's face. "You're lying. Trying to piss me off for disobeying your order to keep away from your fiancée. And all because I have a brain and an opinion about what I want for my life."

"You were born into the wrong family if you want to call the shots in your life. And I'm not lying. You're going to The Fellowship in four days."

"We'll fucking see about that." Shaw marches toward the door and yanks it open, slamming it closed on her way out.

"That's the reason that I forbid her from seeing you. I knew she would behave like a brat."

"She's upset, and she has every right to be. No one wants to be told what they must do, and even more so when it involves marriage and sex. I bet you didn't react well to being told you must marry me."

"I damn sure wasn't happy, but I didn't throw a temper tantrum."

"She's an eighteen-year-old girl who has been with her mother her whole life. You're a twenty-eight-year-old man who was taken from your mother and reared by your father and grandfather to become a powerful leader. Big difference."

"True, and Mum has coddled her. I love Shaw, but she can be a brat when she doesn't get her way."

"She's the baby and the only daughter with four older brothers. I'd be shocked if she weren't spoiled and bratty."

"Enough about Shaw. There are more pressing things to discuss." Kieran takes my hand in his and tugs. "Come. We need to talk."

We need to talk. Nothing good has ever followed those words.

I sit next to Kieran on the bed, and he cups his hands around mine. "Two Order women were killed and dumped on the steps of our compound tonight. Some of the brothers have come forth and placed blame on The Fellowship. They demand blood."

"The Fellowship didn't do that. You have to make them understand that it had to have been another brotherhood; neither Thane nor Sin would have ordered that." It's not our way.

"It wasn't another brotherhood. It was The Order."

"Are you sure?" I know The Order is ruthless, but that would mean that they killed two of their own women to frame The Fellowship. That takes a special kind of evil.

"The stupid fuckers who dumped the bodies were caught on camera. We've not identified them, but we've studied the video. One of them was inked in the space behind his ear with the mark of The Order."

"These people are monsters." And I'm going to be married to the man who leads them. What if he and his father can't reform them? That's more than a little frightening.

"A plan has been set into motion to reveal the traitors before the entire brotherhood. It's happening tomorrow night."

"Good. They deserve everything they get."

"Something else to discuss. I asked, or rather I told, The Fellowship that I wanted three days with you and Ellison so that I could choose which one of you I wanted as my wife. Technically, that time won't be up until Monday night, but I'm taking you back early."

I don't understand. He's claimed me as his mate. "Why?"

"I need you to be in a safe place when our plan plays out, and that's not here."

"What's going to happen?" Kieran looks at me, saying nothing. Looking so torn. "I'm not the enemy."

"It's not that I don't trust you."

"Then what is it?"

"I wanted more time for you to come to know me before I told you who I am to my brotherhood. And what I do." He has that same pained expression as he had this morning.

"Are you talking about your contribution to the brotherhood?"

"Aye."

"I'm not a stranger to contributions and what they are."

"Sinclair is a lawyer. Mitch is an accountant. Jamie is a doctor. I'm none of those things."

"I never thought you were." Kieran grimaces and lowers his face, breaking our eye contact. "Whatever it is, you can tell me. I promise it'll be okay."

He lifts his face and our eyes connect again. "I'm an assassin. I have one job, and it's to kill anyone who becomes a problem for the brotherhood."

Fuck.

That's not what I expected to hear.

"This morning's killing wasn't unplanned? You went there to gun down those men?"

"They were a problem for us, and I took care of them."

"And you're going to take care of the men who killed those women and dumped them here to frame The Fellowship?"

"I am, along with anyone else who tries to be an obstacle in setting this brotherhood on a better course. Tomorrow night could turn into a bloodbath, but no Order member will walk away unclear about the way this brotherhood is going to function going forward."

"You've killed a lot of people?"

I hate hearing that question, but I won't lie to her. "Yes."

"How many?"

"I don't keep a count because it's better if I don't know." Some brothers are proud of their kills. They proudly display the numbers with ink on their skin. I've never understood that.

"How long have you been doing it?"

"My first kill was ten years ago."

Only eighteen when he took his first life. Still a kid. "Killing bothers you." I could see how deeply affected he was when he returned from shooting those men.

"I'm not immune to taking lives. If I ever am, then I've become a savage animal who should be put down."

I'm surprised by how much those words disturb me. "Don't say that."

"An executioner is always in danger of losing his empathy and humanity. I don't want to become that person."

"I won't let that happen."

"My question for you is this: can you accept a killer as your husband?"

"You aren't defined by your contribution." I lean forward and place a kiss against his lips. "I will accept you as my husband just the way you are."

"I'm a dreadful person who does vile things." He closes his eyes and presses his forehead to mine. "I don't deserve you."

I slide off the side of the bed and crawl on top of him, one leg on each side of his hips, and wrap my arms around his shoulders. I want to make him forget about who he is and what he does. "Let's not talk about it anymore." I move my hips and grind against his growing erection. "In fact, let's spend the rest of the night not talking at all."

KIERAN and I are already in the backseat when Ellison is escorted out to join us. She immediately reaches out to me for a hug. "Oh my God, Wes. I'm so relieved that you're in this car."

Not one word is said by anyone during the drive home. I can't bring myself to talk to Kieran in a casual manner in front of Ellison. And I also can't speak to Ellison as though I'm still a captive in front of Kieran. I hide my left hand from Ellison beneath my leg; it's a precarious predicament.

Kieran may be silent, but his possessive hold on my thigh speaks volumes. It tells me how much he hates taking me back. How much he's going to hate being apart for the next few days. And I feel the same.

Lennox phoned Thane to tell him that Kieran was bringing us home, and I'm not surprised to see The Fellowship council standing in front of the house, awaiting our return.

The car stops, and I expect Ellison to jump out and run to Jamie. But she doesn't. Not even when Niall opens the door. Kieran looks at me and then to her. "You're free to go, Miss MacAllister."

Ellison slides over and gets out of the car, but I stay behind. "Come on, Wes. Let's go."

"Miss Breckenridge and I need a private moment. She'll join you in a minute." Ellison doesn't move. "Go, Miss MacAllister. Now."

Kieran motions for Niall to shut the door. The instant it closes, he pulls me into his arms. "I don't want to leave without you. It feels wrong."

"I don't want to be separated from you either." I had no idea I could develop an attachment to someone so quickly.

"I'm coming for you in three days, and I'm not leaving Fellowship property without you."

"I'll be ready." He holds the sides of my face and kisses me like crazy. Like he may never see me again. "Until Wednesday, Kieran."

He kisses my forehead. "Until Wednesday. Call me if you need anything. Anything at all."

"I will."

Kieran taps on the window and Niall opens the door. Jamie races toward me when he sees me leave the sedan. My brother pulls me against him and uses his body to shield me from Kieran's sight. "Are you okay?"

"I'm fine, Jamie."

Kieran lowers his window. "We'll contact you in three days to set up the next meeting."

"Bye," I silently mouth.

"Everyone inside. Bleu and Isobel are desperate to see Westlyn and Ellison," Thane says.

Isobel gives me the *we will talk later eyes* before she hugs me. "Thank God ye came back tae us safely. The entire brotherhood has been in a state of chaos."

"I understand it's the last thing either of you feel like doing right now, but the council needs to question you about the abduction." Thane is eager to get answers for his questions.

Isobel releases her hold on me. "Can they wait until tomorrow? It's late, and both of them are exhausted."

Thane doesn't know it yet, but I have no intentions of being questioned now or later.

Thane looks at Ellison. "Is that what you want? To come back for debriefing tomorrow instead of getting it over with tonight?"

"I haven't slept. I'd probably be more help if we waited since I'm not sure I'm thinking straight right now."

Poor Ellison. I hate so badly that she was a wreck while I was having the time of my life.

"Can you give them something for sleep?" Bleu asks.

I'm not surprised. Bleu was abducted and held captive by Kieran's uncle not long ago. She had a lot of trouble sleeping after she came home.

"I have some mild sedatives at the infirmary."

Jamie can keep his sleeping pills. "Nothing for me. I don't need anything but a bed."

"You're sure? You could take half if you don't want to be fully sedated."

"Positive."

"Westlyn needs her rest, and I'm sure she'll do that best at her flat. I'll see her home." Isobel is dying to get me alone so that she can ask what happened.

Thane puts his arms around me. "I'm sorry we didn't protect you. It's unforgivable."

"Don't give it another thought; I'm fine."

Thane pulls away and looks at my face. "You're fine?"

"I was treated very well by the Hendry family. Like one of their own." Because I am one of their own.

"That's not the impression I got from the oldest son."

Oh, Kieran. What did you say to my family during that meeting?

"I don't know what Kieran said to give you that impression, but he was good to me. No need for a debriefing. Nothing to tell."

I can see that I've shocked Thane. "Well, that changes things."

"I'm exhausted. Am I free to go home?"

"Of course." He hugs me once more. "We're very glad to have you home safely."

Isobel is silent until we get into her car. "Eventful weekend, aye?"

"That's a total understatement."

"Are ye a claimed woman?"

"I am a *very* claimed woman."

Her smile is broad. "Are ye a *happily* claimed woman?"

"I'm very happy."

"Oh, darlin', I'm thrilled tae hear that. It was everything ye hoped for?"

"Everything and more." I bite my bottom lip, trying to hide my grin. "So much more."

"That's wonderful. You really like Lennox's son?"

"I do, and I don't understand how. He kidnapped me. Threatened me. Manhandled me. I wanted nothing more than to see him dead. And then I wanted nothing more than to see him naked."

"He's a very handsome man."

"So sexy." That body… and the things he does with it.

"Just like his father."

Isobel said that she'd known Lennox for a long time. I think something may have gone on between them. "Yes, Kieran definitely looks a lot like his father."

"The claiming went well?"

Well doesn't even begin to describe it. "Maybe too well. I didn't want Kieran to bring me back early."

"Why did he bring ye back early?"

"There's trouble within The Order, and they mean to end it tonight. He felt I would be safer here while they tend to business."

"His decision to bring ye home tae protect ye is a wise one. It shows that he's more concerned with yer safety than with his image."

I hadn't thought of that.

"Are ye going to tell Thane that ye have been claimed?"

"No. I don't want it to cause unnecessary problems." Jamie would flip the fuck out if he knew that Kieran had officially claimed me before the marriage treaty was finalized. "I'm planning to keep things uncomplicated. I'll simply volunteer to be the treaty bride."

"Ye dinnae think yer motive will be questioned?"

"Maybe, but I'll just say that Ellison isn't Fellowship, and this isn't her responsibility. If anyone says anything about Evanna, I'll explain that I want to protect my sister. I'm confident that I won't be drilled about it."

"Sounds like ye have a solid plan."

"I want to thank you for going to Lennox and Kieran after their meeting with the council. Everything you said to Kieran changed the path that he and I have taken together."

"I'm glad it has worked oot for the best. I love ye and I want tae see ye happy."

"I don't know Kieran yet, but I think we can be happy together. We've both agreed to try. We want this marriage to be real."

"That's a better start than some of us get."

Isobel drops me off at my flat, and the first thing I do is shower and prepare for bedtime. I lie in bed watching television, typically one of my favorite shows, but my head isn't in it. I turn off the television and lie there tossing and turning for what feels like forever.

No way I'm going to be able to sleep.

Kieran dropped me off six hours ago. I'm certain that whatever happened with The Order members has gone down. And I don't know if he's dead or alive.

I'm losing my mind with worry for him.

I'm losing my mind with lust for him.

I know it's irrational, and I don't understand how it's possible, but I miss Kieran. I want to be with him. I want him beside me. But those aren't the only irrational feelings I'm having.

Kieran stole me… and I liked it.

He told me I was beautiful… and I liked it.

He took my virginity… and I liked it. A lot.

He calls me wife… and I *love* it.

Captor becomes intended becomes lover becomes husband. Something is very wrong with that picture. And something is very wrong with me for being okay with it.

Maybe I'm just fucked up in the head from being raised by a monster for a father. A stupid woman who's desperate for love and affection from a man, and he's the first to show me any.

Maybe I'm dick-obssesed. Because I damn sure can't stop thinking about Kieran's and when I'm going to get it inside me again.

Maybe I have Stockholm syndrome. Captive falls in love with her captor. He steals the woman, but in the process, he also steals her heart. That's a thing. Perhaps a mental disorder, but still a thing.

Doesn't matter what kind of fucked-up label you put on me, I want him.

I pick up my phone and scroll through my favorites list. Kieran placed his contact at the top. And I love that he labeled himself as *My Intended*. It's sweet.

I don't want to interrupt him while he's busy taking care of problems, but I want to know that he's okay. I need to know. Being in the dark about his safety is killing me.

Westlyn: I'm worried. Please let me know you're OK when you can.

His reply is immediate.

Kieran: All is well. Overseeing cleanup. Almost done.

Cleanup. That means he killed people tonight. He's going to be troubled by what he's done. In pain. His soul, tortured.

I think he needs me. I want him to need me. And I know that I need him.

Westlyn: Come to me. Let me help you shut everything off for a while.

One minute goes by. And another. Three more and no reply.

Have I pushed too hard? Too fast? Maybe I shouldn't have reached out and suggested that he'd have a need to shut everything off. Maybe he'll see that as my calling him weak.

Kieran: Be there in 30.

I sigh with relief.

Westlyn: I'll be waiting.

CHAPTER THIRTEEN
KIERAN HENDRY

WESTLYN BRECKENRIDGE. She could have used this time away from me to try and figure out a way to avoid our reunion. She could have run away and escaped her fate as my wife. But she didn't. Instead, she has reached out to me at a time when I need her most. I think she may understand me better than I understand myself.

I don't want to retreat into myself to that lonesome place. I want to retreat into her. Make her my refuge from my wicked evildoings.

Fuck, I need her.

This woman. She's the light to my dark. The angel to my devil. The quiet to my storm. The key to my prison.

She opens the door when I arrive at her flat, and I say nothing when I enter and take her in my arms. I hold her tightly, breathing in her scent as though my body might absorb some of her goodness and make me less murderous and vile.

I need this—her—in my life so fucking much.

I lessen my hold and pull away, so I can hold her face in my hands. Look at her eyes. "You're the angel who possesses the power to ease my hell."

She comes up on her tiptoes and presses a kiss to my mouth before taking my hand in hers. "Come with me."

I follow her into her bedroom. Lit candles are twinkling around the room, their illuminations waltzing with one another on the walls. A soft croon is coming from the corner of the room—not a song that I know, but it's clearly meant for lovers.

I stop in the middle of Westlyn's bedroom and pull her against me, my hand on her lower back. "Dance with me." She smiles and places one of her tiny hands on my shoulder while the other cups inside mine at our chests. Her body leans against mine and together we move to a song that sounds like making love in the form of music. I've never danced with a woman this way. But I like it.

The song ends, and another begins. Another soft, romantic tune.

I grasp Westlyn's chin and lift, forcing her to look at me. "I want to lose myself in you. Forget the blood and gore and carnage."

She nods. "You can have me any way you need me."

I tug her toward the bed, and she follows without hesitation. We're standing at the bedside when she glides her hands up my chest, pushes my jacket from my shoulders, and tosses it to the chair in the corner. She moves to my tie next, sliding the knot down. I reach for my top button but she stills my hand.

"I want to undress you." She brings my fingers to her mouth, kissing them. "I want to do everything for you tonight." And you will, doll, as long as I ultimately remain in control. I can't ever lose control.

The last button of my shirt is unfastened, and I think she's done until she moves to my cufflinks. Times like this, I hate wearing these kinds of clothes. It would be so much simpler to pull a T-shirt over my head, drop a pair of jeans, and get down to shagging.

A jeans and T-shirt guy... that's not who I am. I'll never be that guy.

Westlyn pushes my shirt from my shoulders and tosses it to the chair to join my jacket. Her mouth drags wet kisses across my chest while her hands explore my pecs. My cock twitches when she bites one of my nipples and then flicks her tongue over it.

She unfastens my pants and lowers the pull tab of the zipper before looking up at me and licking her lips. My cock strains to be released. To get to her. Inside her.

She comes up on her tiptoes and presses a kiss to my mouth. Her plump pink lips, a hint of sweet wine still lingering, taste delicious against my mouth. I can't help but wonder what it would feel like to have them wrapped tight around my cock.

I kick out of my shoes when her hands slide into the sides of my pants and boxer briefs. I almost wince when she grips my hips, digging her nails into my flesh.

My intended takes her time undressing me, looking at and touching almost every inch of my body. It's both agony and delight. Every muscle in my body is tense as sexual desire slowly eclipses restraint. This woman is driving me mad and pushing me beyond the edge of self-control.

I love kissing Westlyn. Enjoying the taste of her mouth. Delighting in the feel of her tongue against mine. But I end our kiss because my cock is greedy. He wants his turn with that pouty mouth.

I take a single step back and sit on the edge of the bed. Looking at Westlyn in that virgin-white nightgown, her nipples pushing through the thin fabric, makes my erection throb. "I want my fiancée to get on her knees and suck my cock."

Fear flashes in her eyes, but it's quickly replaced with fiery passion.

My cock twitches when she lowers herself to the floor and kneels before me. Grasping the back of her head, I pull her closer. I grab my dick at the base and rub it back and forth across her bottom lip, spreading the milky white fluid. "Lick it."

She looks up at me with hooded, submissive eyes, and the tip of my dick trickles more pre-cum. I'm filled with ecstasy when she doesn't hesitate to obey my command. She licks it again and again without even being told to.

I massage the back of her neck, giving her praise. "Such a good lass. Now put it in your mouth and suck."

She opens wide and takes the head into her mouth, bobbing up and down my length. Her tongue is soft, wet, and sensual against the underside of my throbbing cock. Her hand moves up my legs and she lightly cups my balls from the bottom, massaging one of them between her fingers. Fucking tingles run up my spine, and I can't contain the moan building at the back of my throat. "Uh... Wes... fuck..."

She briefly breaks off and licks her lips before taking it into her mouth again, this time so deeply that she gags and tears stream down her face. But she doesn't stop. And I'm captivated by the sight of my dick in her mouth.

Her mouth feels amazing, but I'm ready to slide into her wet pussy. Because that's where babies are made. "I don't want to come in your mouth." She instantly stops on command. I love the way she obeys without hesitation. Such a good girl.

"Take off your gown." And she does. She's not wearing knickers, so she's completely bare for me to look at after the gown is gone. "I can't believe that you're mine. That I get to have you for the rest of our lives."

I want to feel her slick juices gliding all over my cock, but not before I taste them. "Lie down on the bed."

She climbs on her bed and lies on her back, knees pressed together. "Spread your legs. I want to look at you."

I stare at her pussy. Despite the dim lighting from the candle, I can see that it's gleaming. Wet and slick, just as I had imagined.

I slide two fingers into her, and the tip of my dick trickles a little when I feel the warm moisture between her legs. Her body responds. The arch in her back deepens, and so does her breathing.

I move to kneel on the bed between her legs, and my mouth dives into her sweet pussy. I flatten my tongue and move it up and down through her center, careful to only graze her clit. I want this to be a slow burn. But she has other plans.

Her hips move in counterpoint against my mouth so my tongue will hit that sensitive spot at the top of her slit. My girl is horny and isn't being timid about going after what she needs. I like her aggressiveness. I think I'll reward her.

I flick my tongue against her clit and then suck it hard. Her hips tilt upward, giving me more of her pussy to lick and suck. And I know in this moment that I own more than just this orgasm I'm about to give her. Westlyn is mine. She has taken my cock, and next she'll take my name. That puts me on top of the fucking world.

I press my mouth between her legs and show her what it means to be mine by alternating sucking and licking and flicking my tongue against her clit. I question if her backbone is going to break with the way she's tilting her hips upward and curling her shoulders so that she can watch my mouth devour her. She caresses the top of my head, and our eyes lock.

Panted breath moving through parted lips. Hooded eyes. Wrinkled brow. I love the *I'm about to come so fucking hard* face she's making. "Oh God..."

She fists my hair, and her hips buck while her body jolts. Wet floods my mouth, and I taste her orgasm. So fucking delicious. I can't help but lap up every drop.

Her panting slows, and her tense muscles become relaxed. That's when I know that her orgasm has come to an end.

I crawl over her and brush my lips against hers before giving her a slow kiss to coax her back to me from whatever blissful place she's gone to. Our kiss is slow and soft and sweet. I do so to offset the commands I gave her earlier about going down on her knees and sucking my dick.

Her eyes flutter, connecting with mine, and I see so much more than flecks of green and brown and gold. I'm looking at my future. My wife. The mother of my children.

I take her hand and bring it to my chest over my heart. "Mo chroí."

She smiles and transfers my hand to her chest. "Mo chroí."

I nestle between her legs and position the tip of my dick at her opening. My erection pulsates with longing when I feel the hot moisture. It's like her pussy is calling my dick home where it belongs.

I slowly sink into her, her walls stretching to accommodate my every inch. Her pussy is paradise, nirvana, and ecstasy all rolled into one. I swear I could stay balls deep inside it forever.

She hooks her ankles behind my back and uses them to coax me in deeper. Not that I really need encouragement. "If you can use me to fuck away your pain, then do it."

Her words permeate my skin and penetrate my heart. "I don't want to do that to you."

"It's okay if you need to. I want to make it better for you."

"I don't want to cause you pain in order to ease my own." I stop moving and cup the side of her face. "Just being here with you like this makes it better."

I slowly pull back and thrust into her gently. Every thrust is methodical and deliberate, making me very aware of the way my cock is stretching her still-virgin-tight pussy.

Her body molds against mine, and we become one. "Ohh… Kieran…" I love the sound of my name on her lips but especially when it's said with so much passion.

I press my forehead to hers. "Tell me that you're mine. Tell me that I'm the only one, and there'll never be another."

Her hands come up and grasp the sides of my face. "I belong to you. Only you. No one else."

My semen-filled balls contract, sending my seed out through my cock and into her womb. My release is powerful, like an explosion. I don't think I've ever come so hard. I wrap my arm around her waist and pin her down, filling her with every drop I have.

My hand finds hers and we move them between our chests. This time we say the words together. "Mo chroí."

I stay inside her until I soften and slide out. "Can I stay with you tonight?"

"I'd like to see you try to leave me."

I roll off her and lie on my back. I pull her body against mine, and she nuzzles her face against my beating heart with her leg thrown over my midsection.

I kiss the top of her head. "Goodnight, doll."

"Goodnight."

I WAKE and I'm wrapped around Westlyn, the complete opposite of the way we were when we fell asleep. Odd. I don't remember waking and shifting into this position at all. Probably because I sleep so well when she's by my side.

She stretches and yawns, wiggling her bum against my cock. I chuckle. "Good mornin' to you."

"Good mornin'." Westlyn laces her fingers through mine and forms a fist with our two hands. "How do you feel?"

"Well rested." No nightmares. No flashbacks of that murderous, bloody scene from last night.

"Me too."

"It's Monday. We need to go to the registrar's office and give notice of our intent to marry." I don't want to wait a single day longer than necessary. "We have to start planning a wedding. One big enough to accommodate guests from three brotherhoods."

"That's a lot of people, but Isobel is the queen of event planning. I know she'll be happy to help."

"What about your mum?"

"You're a leader. My mum will be over-the-moon happy about this wedding, but warning: she's pretentious. She likes everything to be over the top."

I'm not a fan of pretentious. "And you don't?"

"Not really."

Westlyn is down to earth and doesn't seem to care how much money we have. It's one of the things I like so much about her. "When will I meet Torrie?"

"I was thinking we'd wait until after your meeting with The Fellowship council, and it's official."

"It's already official. The Fellowship council just doesn't yet know that it's official."

"I've been thinking about the meeting, and I think we don't tell the council that you've already claimed me."

"No fucking way. I won't risk this falling through." All of this is fucking with my nerves. I won't rest until I know that my bairn is inside her.

"It won't fall through. We would tell them the truth if it looked like it was. I just think it would go a long way with the council to hear that you didn't force anything."

"I didn't force you to do anything. You freely gave yourself to me."

"That's not what I mean. I think it would cause less strife if they have the impression that you're going to claim me *after* the treaty agreement. I think they'll feel more respected, and that's good for everyone involved."

"I don't want to go into this meeting and even entertain the idea of marrying Ellison or your sister." That would feel so wrong.

"You won't. I'm going to step forward and volunteer."

She didn't just now come up with this idea. "You have all of this already figured out, don't you?"

"I know Thane and Sin and Jamie. Trust me. This is the way this should be handled for a smooth transaction."

My wife-to-be has a head for managing brotherhood affairs. She's highly intelligent. Reminds me so much of Mum.

"I don't like it. I'm used to taking whatever I want, but I'll do this for you because it's the way you'd like it to go. I want you to be happy."

"And I want you to be happy."

"Mmm… I know one thing that would make me very happy."

"I bet it's the same thing that would make me very happy."

Westlyn releases my hand and I move it to cup her between her legs. "What about this?"

"You're moving in the right direction."

I roll my hips and rub my growing erection against her bum. "We haven't done it from behind."

"We also haven't done it with me on top."

Both of those sound good to me. "Which one do you want to try?"

She giggles. "I want to ride you." I roll to my back and Westlyn crawls over me, straddling my hips. "I may not know what I'm doing."

"You're a smart girl. I bet you can figure it out."

She lowers her upper body and kisses the side of my neck, sucking the skin into her mouth. Her hips grind in a circular motion against my hardening cock "Does that feel good?"

I grasp her hips, digging my fingertips into the fleshy meat. "Fuck yeah."

She sits up straight and arches her back, finding my erection with her hand to guide it inside her opening. "I'm going to fuck this dick so hard."

Westlyn and I both jolt when we hear a woman's scream. "Westlyn Breckenridge! What are you doing?"

She rolls off me to her back and yanks the sheet up to cover both of us. "How did you get into my flat?"

"I have a key."

"What are you doing here?

"Evanna told me you came home early. I'm here to check on you since you didn't even have the courtesy to let me know you were back."

"I'm sorry. A lot has happened the last few days."

"Please tell me that you've not allowed this man to ruin you." The woman rubs her forehead. "Oh God. No Fellowship man is going to have you now. Even if Thane bribes him."

I don't care for the way this woman is speaking to Westlyn. "That's enough of that."

"Who are you to decide what's enough?"

"I'm to be her husband, so when I say it's enough… it… is… enough."

She sneers. "Her husband? I don't think so. She is a Breckenridge. Her marriage will be an advantageous one—not to some nobody who's not even part of the brotherhood."

"Mother…"

"Has he tainted you?"

The woman can see that I'm naked. Westlyn's naked. We aren't teenagers playing around in the sack. What does she think we're doing?

"It isn't possible for a husband to taint his wife." My mother-in-law-to-be looks at me through narrowed eyes, obviously not appreciating my mention of us as husband and wife.

"I can't believe you brought a man here. If anyone knows you've lost your virginity, it's over." Her mother walks the floor, her hand pinching her chin while she mutters words beneath her breath. "When you marry, we'll have to schedule your wedding during your cycle. Maybe, just maybe, we can fool your husband into believing it's virginal blood."

"Stop, Mother. Kieran has claimed me, and I'm going to marry him."

"Kieran… Kieran Hendry?" There's no mistaking the instant delight on her face. "The new up-and-coming leader of The Order?"

"Aye, that would be me."

She places her palms together and brings them to her face to hide her grin. "My daughter is marrying a leader. That is wonderful news."

"I need you to keep quiet about it until after the meeting with the council."

She laughs. "Why in the world would I do that? My daughter is marrying a leader. I want to tell everyone."

"We don't want the council to know that he's claimed me before the terms of the treaty have been agreed upon. It could cause problems."

"Oh, we definitely don't want problems. I won't say a word to anyone."

I don't like this woman. I want her gone. "We were in the middle of trying to seal our bond."

Westlyn punches me. "Kieran…"

"Say no more. I'm out of here." She stops in the doorway and looks back. "It needs to be a boy."

Well, at least we agree upon that much.

"Mother… get out."

I've been away from Westlyn for two days. I don't like it one bit. I'm ready to bring my intended home where she belongs. And I'm about to do just that.

It doesn't feel right walking into this meeting with The Fellowship council to ask for Westlyn's hand. It's like asking for something that already belongs to me. And I'm not accustomed to asking for anything. I take what I want. Just like I took her and made her mine.

But I understand the point she's making about playing nice with The Fellowship. They aren't a brotherhood you should provoke, hence one of the reasons we are seeking an alliance. I can be a cocky bastard, but even I know that you don't want The Fellowship as an enemy.

My father and I enter the dining room where The Fellowship council, Westlyn, and Ellison are waiting. My eyes immediately go to my intended, like a magnet to steel. I can't not look at her. She's so fucking beautiful, it hurts. I can't believe the misery I've endured while we've been apart.

"Gentlemen. Please join us," Thane says, but I barely hear him. I'm too enthralled by Westlyn.

I take the seat beside her, and I fight the urge to reach out and kiss her pouty pink lips—the lips that were wrapped tightly around my dick, sucking me so hard, only a couple of nights ago.

"Have you come to a decision about the treaty?" my father asks. I hear the words decision and treaty in the same sentence, and my attention is captured. This is it. We're about to see if Isobel was right.

Thane's answer will determine if I walk out of here with a wife, or engage in the biggest fight I've ever fought. War.

"Aye. We are pleased to say that we have decided to accept. Westlyn has offered herself to be Kieran's wife—if that's agreeable with him."

Westlyn has offered herself to be Kieran's wife. There has never been a sentence to make me any happier. "Aye. I'm agreeable to taking Westlyn as my wife." More than agreeable, I'm fucking elated.

"I think Kieran and Westlyn will make a good match," my father says. He's wrong. I already know that we make a perfect match. "And your decision on who will be taking Shaw as a wife?"

"I will," Mitch says.

No surprise there. Westlyn said that Jamie wouldn't do it. Fine by me. He and I aren't on the best of terms right now. I can handle him being my wife's brother, but I'm not keen on him being my sister's husband. Especially when he's been fucking the MacAllister woman.

"Very good." My father is pleased with Mitch's decision; he's the one Dad wanted for Shaw anyway. The second son of a leader, same as him. He knows Mitch will have a good standing within his brotherhood. Shaw's place within The Fellowship will be solid.

"Kieran and Westlyn will notify the district registrar tomorrow of their intent to wed." Already done. "Do we agree that the wedding will take place in four weeks?"

"No objection from us," Thane says.

My father's plan couldn't have worked better. I get a beautiful wife… one who loves to fuck. A wife who sucks my cock. A wife who sees my pain and wants to make it better. She's perfect for me. I couldn't ask for more.

I'm going to be happy with her. And it's such a surprise. I never expected that. We could really fall in love.

"Kieran will claim Westlyn tonight unless there are any objections." I can't stop the grin spreading across my face. I probably look like a teenage boy who's about to get his first grope of a girl's tits.

Thane flicks his hand in the direction of the empty chair. "I see only one bride here for exchange."

I was waiting for someone to point out my sister's absence. I hope her obstinate behavior doesn't affect Thane's decision to let me take Westlyn with me today. I'm not leaving this compound without her.

"My apologies for Shaw's absence. I'm afraid she needs a little more time to adjust to the idea of marrying someone she's never met. She is a Hendry and will fulfill her duty. I will see to it personally." I hope my father's promise is enough to satisfy the council today.

"Shaw isn't the only one marrying a stranger she's never met. It would have been a nice gesture for her to at least come meet the man volunteering to take her." Mitch's voice is laced with frustration.

I can't say that I blame him. He came here expecting to leave with a bride.

My father clears his throat. "It is my solemn vow that Shaw will be delivered to Mitch by the end of the week."

My father's statement makes me nervous as fuck. I'm not sure that he is going to be able to make good on it. Not with the way Shaw is behaving. And if he does, I fear she'll be difficult to handle once she's in the hands of The Fellowship.

"Your daughter clearly isn't onboard with being a treaty bride." Mitch has no idea how right he is.

"Shaw is young. Headstrong. She has her own ideas about what she wants for her life, but I will steer her in the right direction." My father has been trying to steer her in the right direction for over a week, and he's not been successful yet.

"The lass sounds obstinate." Mitch doesn't know the half of it. "I don't want a difficult wife."

"I admit my daughter is stubborn, but she isn't unbending. I swear to you, Mitch, that you won't find a more beautiful wife within The Fellowship or The Order. And she is pure. Arabella and I have ensured that she will be a virgin on her wedding night. You won't be disappointed with her."

The conflict in Mitch's eyes is real. No one understands it more than I do—but he'll marry Shaw because it's his duty as the son of a leader. "I will go through with the marriage."

Thane turns steely eyes back to my father. "Deliver Shaw to us by Friday; otherwise, the agreement is off, and we will expect Westlyn to be returned."

Hate it for The Fellowship, but that's not going to happen. I will not return Westlyn again. Ever.

"We want this treaty, Thane. Probably more than you do. I give you my word that Shaw will be here."

"Then this meeting is adjourned."

This meeting went much more smoothly than expected. Jamie didn't make any arguments about my taking his sister. Probably because his lover would be one of my alternatives and he doesn't want to give her up.

"Wait. I need to know what this means for my sister." I should have known Jamie wasn't going to let me walk out of here with his sister without saying something.

I reach for Westlyn's hand. "She is my mate and will leave with me when we go. I'm claiming her tonight."

He hates this outcome. I see it in the pained expression on his face. Just as I will hate giving Shaw to Mitch. "I need a few minutes with my sister in private."

"You can have as many minutes as you like, but Westlyn is mine. It's been decided." Even more so than you know. There's no going back.

"You haven't delivered your end of the bargain, and you've not officially claimed her. Nothing is in stone yet."

That's where you are oh so wrong, brother-in-law. I've claimed Westlyn. Made her mine forever. She may already have our firstborn inside her as we speak.

I open my mouth to tell Jamie how wrong he is, but I see Westlyn's pleading eyes begging me to not say anything.

I'm not one to back down from a challenge, and that's exactly what Jamie is doing—challenging me. It's hard as fuck, but I concede for her.

I release Westlyn's hand, and she follows her brother into the hallway. The fucker is going to try to convince her to not leave with me. I know it. But his arguments are useless. Westlyn wants me as much as I want her.

It's unpleasant sitting at the conference table with The Fellowship council in silence. We're going to be allies. We should be able to have a civil conversation. "I know everyone around this table loves Westlyn, and I'd like you to know that I will treat her well."

"You'd better," Sinclair says.

I don't care for the ultimatum I hear in his voice. "Just as Mitch had better treat Shaw well." This is a two-way street.

"You don't have to worry. I will be good to your sister." Westlyn tells me that Mitch is one to keep his temper. He demonstrates that in his statement. That's good. Because I have a feeling that Shaw is going to push him to, and probably beyond, those limits.

"Westlyn speaks highly of you. She has eased many of my concerns about your marrying my sister."

"Well, no one has eased our concerns about Westlyn marrying you." Ellison has found her voice.

"We spent two days together, and then she volunteered to marry me. I don't think she'd have done that if things hadn't gone well between us."

"You raped her."

"I did no such thing." I see the disbelief on Ellison's face. "Ask her yourself if you don't believe me."

My father gets up from the table. "I think Westlyn and her brother have had plenty of time to talk."

I couldn't agree more. We open the door and step into the hallway. Jamie hugs Westlyn, and I don't mistake the daggers I see in his eyes when he looks at me. "I love you, Wes."

"I love you too."

I'm taking Westlyn again, this time with the consent of her brotherhood. In their eyes, I will be officially claiming her tonight.

It's done.

She is mine.

CHAPTER FOURTEEN
KIERAN HENDRY

"WE DID IT, DOLL." I cup my hands around Westlyn's face and pull her in for a kiss. She tastes sweet and fruity and pungent. "Mmm… someone has had wine."

"I drank a few glasses to calm my nerves. I was nervous something would go wrong."

"No need to be nervous. I told you that there was no way I was leaving without you."

"I know, but I worried Jamie might do something crazy." She had every right to worry about that one.

"You mean do something crazy like pull out his Glock and point it at my face?"

Westlyn twists her body for a better look at me. "How do you know he carries a Glock?"

"Because he pulled it out and pointed it between my eyes."

"What?" Her voice rises. "When?"

"At the first marriage treaty meeting." I shrug. "It was nothing."

"It's *not* nothing. My brother pointed a gun at your face."

I shot him first. I'm probably lucky that he didn't put a bullet in me. "He didn't shoot me, so that makes it nothing. Wasn't the first time that's ever been done and it won't be the last."

"I don't like hearing things like that. Reminds me of the danger that you're in."

"Goes along with this way of life, and being in a leadership role increases the danger." I'm always going to be targeted.

"I know, but I'd rather not be reminded. And I'd prefer that my brother and husband didn't shoot, or threaten to shoot, each other anymore."

"I promise I won't shoot your brother again… as long as he doesn't try to take you from me." If that happens, I will be forced to put a bullet in him.

"He isn't going to take me from you." She sounds confident.

"Is that what you talked about in the hallway?"

"Yes."

"What did he say to you?"

"That I didn't have to marry you to save Ellison because they had a plan. And that he would find a good match for me… a man I could love."

Jamie is a good brother for wanting Westlyn to be happy. I don't begrudge him for that. I want the same for Shaw. "And you said?"

"That I wanted to marry you."

"I bet he didn't like that much."

She giggles. "He didn't love it."

"Everything is going to be fine, doll. He'll see how well I treat you, and then he's going to be okay with our union."

"Your threat to possibly take Ellison as a wife forced his hand. He claimed her after you brought us home. They've notified the district registrar of their intent to marry. They were notifying Thane and Sin after the meeting."

My brother-in-law should be thanking me for kidnapping his lover and giving him the push he needed to go after the woman he wants and loves.

"He'll have to go through endurance?"

"Yes, and I'm terrified for him."

If Fellowship endurance is anything like The Syndicate's, Jamie Breckenridge is about to take a fucking beating. That sucks.

I can't take away her fear, but I can reassure her that all will eventually be okay. "It'll be worth it when he has his woman. Just like kidnapping you and risking war with The Fellowship was worth it because I have you now."

"You say really sweet things sometimes. I wouldn't have thought that was possible when we first met."

It's a first for me. "I've never had to be sweet to a woman before. But you make me want to be sweet to you."

"And what if I want you to be rough with me?"

"What kind of rough are we talking?"

The car comes to a stop at the compound. "We'll talk about it later."

"Aye, we certainly will."

We enter the house through the front entrance, and Mum calls out for me from the living room. "It's me."

"Come in here." She's been nervous about this meeting, so afraid something would go wrong.

Mum and Shaw are all smiles when they see Westlyn at my side. "Oh thank God."

"All went well. No troubles." I look at Shaw. "Other than them being upset that their treaty bride was a no-show."

Shaw crosses her arms and frowns. She looks like such a brat when she does that. "Well, they can just keep on being upset."

"You should have at least made an effort and gone to meet your husband."

"There was no way they were going to let me leave if I had gone. And he's not my husband."

Mitch seems like a reasonable person. I think he would have allowed Shaw to leave. "He was disappointed that you weren't there. He's eager to meet you."

"I bet he is."

Westlyn takes her phone out of her purse. "Would you like to see a picture of him?"

"No."

Westlyn thumbs through photos on her phone. "Are you sure? He's very good-looking. Fit and easy on the eyes."

I'd be jealous if Mitch weren't her cousin. Shaw's mouth pulls to the side, her nose scrunches, and she shrugs. "I... guess." She comes to Westlyn and leans close for her first look at her husband-to-be.

"What do you think?"

She suppresses a smile. Little shite likes what she sees. There's promise yet. "You're right. He is handsome."

"We were raised more like siblings than cousins. I know almost everything about Mitch. I can tell you anything you want to know about him." Westlyn flips through several more photos. "Here he is playing with the babies. I think it's my favorite picture of him."

I like what Westlyn is doing with my sister. Building Mitch's character in Shaw's eyes. But she needs to do it later. I'm ready to get her under me.

I wrap my arms around Westlyn from behind. "You and Shaw can continue this conversation tomorrow."

My mum grins. "It's been a long, stressful day. I'm sure the two of you would like to retire early."

"Retiring early? That's what we're calling it these days?"

At first I think Shaw is being her typical cheeky self, but her giggle lets me know that she's jesting. I think getting a look at her intended and approving of him has improved her mood.

"Maybe we can have lunch together tomorrow? I'm eager to get to know you both." I love that Westlyn wants to get to know my mum and sister.

"I think that's a lovely idea." Mum comes to Westlyn and kisses the side of her face. "I'm very happy that everything went well today. Glad to have you back."

"I'm happy to be back too."

Not as happy as she's going to be. I think about all the things I'm going to do to Westlyn when I get her in my bed, and my dick gets so hard that it's difficult to walk. My suite feels a million miles away.

I shut the door behind us and lock it… just in case. Our fun has been interrupted too many times.

She stops before reaching the bed and turns to look at me. I grab the knot of my tie and slowly drag it downward while I eye fuck her. "I love the way you look tonight." The tight black dress hugs her curves perfectly, showing off her full breasts, small waist, and round bottom. And the heels… fuck, they stretch her legs for miles.

"I'm glad you like it. I wore it just for you."

Fuck yeah, she wore it for me. I slip my jacket off and toss it toward the chair, coming nowhere near making it. Fuck it.

"You wore it for me. Now take it off for me." She moves her hands behind her back and lowers the zipper to her waist. The fabric over both shoulders falls, revealing the most perfect pair of tits in a black lace push-up bra. "Wiggle out of the dress... slowly. And leave the heels on."

I untuck my shirt and work on unbuttoning it, beginning at the top, while she pushes her dress down her hips and legs. My shirt and her dress hit the floor at the same time. She kicks out of the fabric and is left only in her heels and black lace lingerie. So fucking hot.

I unfasten the button on my pants and lower the zipper. "Take off your bra. I want to see your tits."

I kick out of my shoes and push my pants down my legs. Bending down to remove my socks, I never take my eyes off her as she unclasps her bra and makes a show of lowering the straps and tossing it aside.

Most gorgeous tits I've ever seen. Perfect size. Perfect shape. Perfect color. So perky for their fullness. And her nipples... when I lick them, they feel like smooth pebbles against my tongue.

We're on even ground with me in my boxer briefs and her in her knickers. My fingers mimic hers, going into her waistband at the same time hers dive into mine. We're like mirror images pushing underwear down our legs. And then we're both standing before each other bare.

Her body in contrast to mine is so different. I'm hard where she's soft. I bulge where she curves. I have hair where she's smooth. Everything about her body is feminine and delicate.

I stare at the Y where her legs meet, and that one little tuft of hair above the slit of her pussy drives me fucking mad. The longer I stand here looking at her naked and in those heels, the harder my cock gets. I have to touch her.

She moves to the bed, lowering her body so that she's lying on her back, knees bent. She watches me through the wide space between her thighs.

I stop when I reach the bed and look at her pussy. It's glistening wet and extra pink and swollen from the increased blood flow. She's ready for me. "Do you like it when I lick you?"

"Yes, I do."

"Do you want me to eat you?"

"Ohh... yes."

I'm not sure who likes it more. Me or her. "I want to hear you say it."

Her cheeks pinken. "I want you to lick my pussy... and eat me out."

I crawl onto the bed and kneel before her, slowly sliding down so my face is buried between her legs. I push her thighs apart and trail my nose up her slit, inhaling her sweet scent. I love the way she smells.

She moans when my tongue moves up and down her center. I lick and suck and munch on her pussy like it's the best meal I've ever had. My mouth slurping her juices makes one of the most obscene noises I've ever heard. Fuck, I love that sound. Makes me even harder.

Her hands fist my hair and her back arches from the bed, shifting her hips so her legs are spread even wider. My mouth explores and tastes everything in between, including her orgasm. "Ohhh... Kieran. I'm coming."

I suck her clit hard once more, finishing her off with a bang, before I crawl up her body. I can't resist taking her hand in mine and bringing both to our chests. This time I don't have to tell her to say it. "Mo chroí," we whisper together.

I kiss her mouth and smile against her lips. "I've been gentle with you the other times, but tonight I want to stretch your pussy. I want to fuck you hard and pound my cock in you so deep that when I come, my seed squirts into the mouth of your womb."

Her breath hitches. "Do it. Fuck me as hard as you want."

I grab her hips and adjust her underneath me, lining her body up so it can take every inch of my cock. I'm so hard that I don't even have to use my hand to guide it to her entrance. I thrust and it slides into her tight, slick hole.

I sink deep into her walls, and they squeeze my cock like magic. Her small pussy wrapped around my dick feels amazing. I move in and out of her, building the pace, my balls slapping against her bum. I love seeing her tits jarred with every thrust.

She rocks her hips, meeting me thrust for thrust, and we increase the speed until we reach high gear. I grab the backs of her thighs and push her legs up so that she's folded in half. She screams with my next thrust. "Oh God. I feel you hitting it."

It. She means her womb. I bore into her like a jackhammer, every plunge forcing a moan of pleasure from her throat. My eyes lock on hers as I give her my full length over and over. Every stroke is symbolic of my claiming this woman as mine.

Her soft sighs and murmurs of pleasure build, and I'm not sure when, but at some point, they become loud moans gradually developing into screams. Some of them include my name. Good thing we're the only ones in this wing of the compound.

I feel my orgasm approaching. I thrust hard and deep, pushing her legs back so I can squirt my hot seed into the opening of her womb. "Tell me how much you want my cum inside you."

"I want it all. Every last drop... inside me."

"Fuck!" My cock thickens, and I tremble as my cum shoots out, filling her with every drop I have in my balls. I ride out the pleasure until I have nothing left to give.

I don't pull out when I'm finished. I want to stay buried inside this woman as long as possible. And keep my semen where it needs to be.

I release her legs and fall on top of her. Exhausted. Sweaty. Empty.

Her arms wrap around my back, and her nails lightly scrape against my skin. We lie that way, saying nothing, until my cock goes completely soft and slides out of her.

I roll off her and lie on my back by her side. "Was I too rough?"

"No. I liked it. It was a nice alternative to making love."

Happy to hear that. "I enjoy slow and sweet, but sometimes a man just needs to feel like a man and fuck hard."

"You can fuck me hard anytime you want."

I had no idea what I was getting when I stole Westlyn. And then I saw her face. I thought she was beautiful, but I still didn't know what I was getting. Now I've made her mine, and I'm only beginning to find out who she is.

An amazing woman. An amazing lover. An amazing wife.

I think she makes falling in love with her very easy.

CHAPTER FIFTEEN

WESTLYN BRECKENRIDGE

"Shaw and I haven't ventured out in Edinburgh much, so we're not familiar with the restaurants. Would you mind choosing for us, Westlyn?"

"I would love to take you to Duncan's. It's The Fellowship drinking hole, but they have a nice choice of pub food." A wrinkle forms across Arabella's forehead. "But we can go somewhere else if you're not comfortable with being around Fellowship members yet."

"Someone has to make the first move. We'll have lunch at Duncan's." She smiles. "And hope that no one spits in our food."

There are more patrons than usual at Duncan's. "Big crowd. They must have some good daily specials."

We're forced to sit at a table in the middle of the pub. Not the one I would have chosen, but we'll take what we can get.

Nessa, one of Leith's new barmaids, is at our table almost instantly. Nice girl. "Any good specials today?"

"The Scottish tapas are delicious. Pan-seared chicken is a close second. Don't get the trout. It's not fresh."

"Tapas and a pint of Guinness for me."

I look over at the triad table—Sin, Leith, and Jamie's special table— and it's empty. A reminder that Jamie is at the infirmary recovering from endurance. Ellison reassures me that he's all right and that she's going to take good care of him, but I still worry.

"Wes…" I instinctively turn when I hear my name, and I nearly choke when I see who it is.

Shite. Shaw is going to think I planned this meeting. No way she won't. I'm certain she'll lose all trust in me now.

I get up and Mitch kisses the side of my face. "Surprised to see you here."

I laugh nervously. "Same here."

Mitch looks at my lunch guests, waiting for an introduction. All color drains from Shaw's face, no doubt because she recognizes Mitch from the photos I showed her last night. "Mitch, this is Arabella and Shaw Hendry."

His eyes go directly to his intended, and he smiles. "Shaw…" He moves toward her and holds out his hand. I sigh with relief when she offers her hand instead of… I don't know what. Shaw's behavior has been so unpredictable that she's capable of just about anything. "This day just got a whole lot better."

Shaw smiles. "That's a nice thing to say."

"Would you care to step outside with me for a moment? I'd love to talk… just the two of us."

Shaw's eyes widen, and she nods. "Okay."

Arabella and I watch Mitch and Shaw walk toward the front door. "I would love to eavesdrop on the conversation those two are about to have. Did you know that Mitch would be here?"

I come here for lunch often, and I've never seen him in here at this time of day. "I had no idea."

"I hope that he says something to bring her to her senses. As much as her father and I have tried, we haven't been able to make her see reason."

Shaw's continued refusal to wed Mitch is going to cause a big problem with The Fellowship. They could stop my marriage and try to take me back. I don't want that. And Kieran won't allow it without a fight. If she doesn't go along with the treaty, there will be a war.

"I thought she was coming around a little last night when she saw the pictures of him." I could tell that she was liking what she saw.

"She did say that he was handsome, but I don't think his physical appearance is going to change her mind. She wants to marry for love."

She looked happy to meet him just now. "She could fall in love with Mitch."

"And you could fall in love with Kieran."

"I'm fairly certain that's already on its way to happening." I look down to hide my embarrassment. "That's crazy, right? We've known each other for five minutes."

"Everything about your relationship with Kieran is on high speed. I don't think it's crazy at all." So many factors have sped up this process.

"When did you know that you loved Lennox?" Or does she love him?

"I was infatuated with him very early on. Before we married. But I don't think I loved him until about halfway through my pregnancy with Kieran."

"How long before he loved you?"

"It happened much sooner for me than for him, but I think that's just a man thing. They're different creatures and don't feel the depths of emotion the way we do."

"I've been surprised by Kieran's behavior. I expected him to be cold-hearted, and he was right after we met, but he's different now. He acts as though he's open to falling in love with me."

"My son is under your spell." I think she's politely saying that he is obsessed with my vagina. And she's right. He is. "Enchanted or capti-vated or whatever you want to call it… it's not a bad place to be at this early point in your relationship."

"I like where things are going with us."

"Kieran likes it too." Arabella looks over my shoulder. "Here she comes… without Mitch."

Shaw takes her seat and battles a smile while saying nothing. She's going to make us ask.

Arabella is on the edge of her seat. "Well?"

"Well what?"

"Stop being a shite and tell me what happened between Mitch and you."

"He's giving me until Sunday evening to come to him on my own. After that, he's coming to the compound to claim me. Well… to collect me. And then I guess he means to claim me."

Wow. That's not what I was expecting out of mild-mannered Mitch.

"What are you going to do?" Not sure why I ask. I know she isn't going voluntarily.

"If he wants me, he'll have to come take me."

"Will you go willingly?" Arabella sounds so hopeful.

"No way. I'm playing hard to get."

Arabella lowers her forehead to her palm. "You are hard to get. There's no playing to it."

"Well, things are different now that we've met and spoken." Her cheeks redden. "He told me that I was the most beautiful woman he'd ever seen."

That catches her mum's attention. "Oh? I'm sure that must have been very flattering to hear from a handsome man."

"No man has ever said anything like that to me." She covers her mouth and giggles. "And he couldn't stop touching me."

"Touching you?" Where did they go that he was freely having body contact with her?

"Nothing out of line. He reached out and took my hand and rubbed his thumb back and forth over the top while he told me what he planned to do. It was nice. I liked it."

Shaw is like me in the respect that she's never gotten much male attention. I'm sure she is flattered by Mitch's interest.

Before last night, Mitch was a faceless name. Then he was only a person in photos who she'd never spoken to. This chance encounter changes everything.

"I think it'll be romantic if Mitch comes and takes me. That's what Dad did with you. And the same with Kieran and Westlyn, except with more force. Both of those instances worked out."

Arabella inhales and releases her breath slowly. "I'm relieved that you're finally accepting Mitch as your fate."

"Well, I'm relieved that he isn't disgusting. He's even better looking in person. And taller than I expected. And more muscular." Sounds like Shaw was noticing every detail about Mitch. "Thank you for bringing us here."

"It was just fate for you two to meet today."

"I think so too."

I spent the day showing Arabella and Shaw around Edinburgh, particularly some of the best places to eat and shop. We even went into a bridal shop and looked at dresses. My mum would be furious if she knew I did that with Arabella instead of her.

I enjoyed our time together. Arabella is so much more pleasant than my mother, and Shaw showed me a new side of her I'd not seen. One I like very much. I think we could be fast friends.

Everything about my new life is good. I didn't know that I could be this happy and with people who were strangers to me not so long ago.

I've heard people say that it's possible to meet someone new and feel like you've known each other for years. That's how I feel about Kieran. Like we've known each other in another life and this isn't our first time meeting.

I feel myself beginning to care for him. It's not love yet, but I feel like that's something that could come easily... especially if we continue to grow closer through physical intimacy.

Every time he touches my body, another part of me becomes his. At the rate we're going, he'll own every part of me by the time we marry.

Only a month until I'm Mrs. Kieran Hendry. I wonder if I'll already be pregnant when I walk down the aisle. Part of me hopes not, but then another part hopes I am so I can please Kieran; I know a baby would make him happy.

A son. An heir. That's what Kieran wants first, and then sweet little girls to adore and spoil. I wonder if there's a way to increase the odds of conceiving a boy. I think that's something I should investigate.

MY HEAD IS TILTED BACK, the water rinsing the conditioner from my hair. My eyes are closed, but I hear the bathroom door open and then close again. "Kieran?"

"It's me. I'm coming in." Amazing how quickly I'm becoming accustomed to living with Kieran and doing everyday domestic things together. Like showering at the same time. God, I love the way his hands feel on me when my skin is wet. It's so much more sensitive and responsive.

"You missed dinner."

"I'm sorry. I had Order business. I should have called." He isn't in his

I just shot and killed some people funk, so I'm guessing he was taking care of another kind of business.

"It's okay, but I would have appreciated a call to let me know you'd be late." I hope that didn't sound like a nag.

He stands behind me and places his hands on my hips, giving me a sweet kiss on the side of my neck. "You're acting like my wife or something."

"I can't imagine why."

He releases me and begins washing his hair. "Not much longer until you walk down the aisle wearing a pretty white dress."

"I looked at wedding dresses today."

"Only looked?"

"My mum and sister will want to be there when I buy my dress. And probably Bleu and Ellison and Lorna as well. Ellison and Shaw will need dresses too. Maybe we can make a girls' day out of it." I know the girls will love Shaw. And she's going to be Mitch's wife. She's becoming part of our girls' group even if she doesn't know it yet.

"I'm not sure that Shaw will need a dress; Mitch is going to call off the whole thing if she keeps acting like a brat."

I can't wait to tell him about today. "Trust me... Shaw will need a dress. Soon."

"Has something happened?"

"I took your mum and Shaw to The Fellowship pub for lunch today. Mitch came in while we were there. He took Shaw outside for a private conversation and told her that she had until Sunday to come to him. If she doesn't, he's coming for her." I've never been prouder of Mitch.

"I would say good for him except that's the worst fucking thing in the world he could have said to her. She hates ultimatums."

"She didn't hate this one. She thinks it's romantic for him to come and take her. And I think he should do it before Sunday. Maybe we take her to Ellison's inception ceremony with us, and he snatches her from there."

"Why would he do that when he doesn't have to?"

"Because she thinks it's romantic to be stolen. I think she'd find it extra romantic if he tells her he couldn't wait until Sunday. She also won't be expecting it, which would be a nice touch." I think Shaw is like me. Deep down she likes a bossy alpha even if she doesn't know it yet. "Shaw is going to be Fellowship. She wouldn't question a request for her presence at the ceremony. It's a perfect opportunity." I'm sure she'd be eager to go so that she can see Mitch again.

"I like your idea a lot. I'll talk to Mum and Dad, and if they approve, I think we should make it happen."

I love that Kieran listens to my ideas and allows me to have a voice. "I'll talk with Mitch as soon as you have your parents' approval."

"This ceremony is coming at a good time. I can use this opportunity to meet your people while they're gathered in one place."

"I should probably schedule a time for you to officially meet my mum and sister before the ceremony."

"Aye, it would be nice to be introduced to your mum while I'm wearing clothes... and not being ridden like a bull."

Oh God. I still can't believe my mum walked in on Kieran and me like that. We weren't doing it... yet, but I was on top of him about to sink down on his dick. So humiliating. But I don't think she cared at all. She was too high about learning that I was going to marry a leader.

"So many people to meet. So much to learn about each other."

We swap places so Kieran can stand under the water. "What would my wife-to-be like to know about me?"

"Everything, but start with what kind of work you do when you're not..." I hate to say killing. "When you're not *solving problems* for the brotherhood?"

His chuckle relieves me. "I'm a numbers guy. I do most of the accounting and bookkeeping. Projections, statistics, etcetera."

He's an accountant? "You're about to be my husband. Why did I not know that about you?"

"I wasn't formally trained. I didn't go to college. I just happen to be good with numbers."

I hear something there in his voice. Regret? Chagrin?

Breckenridge men have higher educations, but I don't want Kieran to believe I see him as less because he didn't pursue that. "College degrees are mostly unnecessary in our world. Being a lawyer or doctor... those kinds of things are the exception. I have a college degree, but a lot of good it's done me."

"I would have liked to have attended college, but I was too busy mastering my skill."

Kill skill. Well, if he's the one doing the killing, then he's not the one being killed. That's the only positive way to look at what he does.

"I'm surprised that Abram allowed you to attend college since a woman typically only continues her education to learn a trade for contribution."

"My education was in childhood practices." It's embarrassing to admit how I talked my father into it. "I was supposed to be learning how to properly mother Sin's children, the future of The Fellowship. That's why my father conceded and allowed me to attend."

Kieran chuckles. "Your education wasn't for nothing. You were learning how to mother *my* children."

"I guess it's a good thing, because I damn sure didn't learn how to parent a child by example." I wonder if Kieran has considered that… that my parenting could mimic the worst parents on earth.

"I'm sure you'll be a wonderful mother."

I want to be a good mother, but I'm not sure I have it in me. "I hope Arabella doesn't mind if I count on her for parenting advice. I sure can't count on mine."

"I'm sure she would love to advise you. My mum was a wonderful mother. She loves babies so much." She must. She had five. "She's excited to have a grandchild. My father is too."

The only reason my mother would be excited for a grandchild is so she can brag about it being the next leader. That's sad. It's also sad to say that the kindest thing she ever did for her children was handing us over to a nanny. She was a horrible mother. But she's still my mother.

"Talking about our baby makes me want to work on it." He wraps his arms around me from behind, filling his hands with my breasts and squeezing. His mouth presses to the side of my neck. "I thought about you, and this, all day. I could hardly add one and one."

I lean into him, feeling his erection against my bum. "I did some research today. I have something for us to try."

He thrusts his pelvis so his hard cock pokes into one of my cheeks. "I like the sound of that."

"But not here. In the bed."

He turns off the water. "By all means."

We move straight to the bed, not taking time to dry off. I place my hand on his chest when we reach the bedside so he'll know to hold up. "Turns out that there are theories about how to conceive a boy."

He grins. "You have my attention."

"Boy sperm needs a shorter distance to swim to the womb in order to win the race. They're weak and die off before crossing the finish line if deposited too far away from the mouth of the womb. Girl sperm is resilient and will soldier on after the boys die." I can't stop my grin. "We need to do it in a position with deep penetration."

Kieran wraps his hand around his erection and slaps it against my stomach. "With a dick like this, all positions involve deep penetration."

He's so proud of his manhood. And he should be. Even though I've not been with anyone else, I still know it's impressive. "Some positions are deeper than others because of my anatomy."

"Deep penetration. Got it."

He moves toward me, and I stop him with my hand again. "Also… I need to come before you. Boy sperm have a better chance at survival if the alkaline secretion released with orgasms is already present."

"You always orgasm before me. Because I'm nice like that." Kieran is a very giving lover. He has made every sexual experience between us pleasurable, which makes me want to do it more and more. Smart move on his part.

"Yes, you are nice like that. And I very much appreciate it."

"I think the first thing on our to-do list is to give you an orgasm."

I sit on the bed and scoot to the middle. He moves over my lower body and moves his nose up and down between my legs, inhaling deeply. "You always smell so good. I can't get enough of this scent."

His mouth devours everything between my legs. Kissing, licking, sucking, nibbling. It's done with meticulous skill. "You are so good at that."

I open my legs wider and he places his thumb at the top of my slit, pulling upward and completely exposing my clit for his tongue. So much more sensitive that way. "That feels amazing."

Kieran inserts his fingers and pumps, rubbing me on the inside with curled fingers. I lift my head from the bed to watch him between my legs. He looks at me and I'm a goner when our eyes meet. "Ohh… uh… ohh." I push my fingers into the top of his hair and tilt my hips up so that he is rubbing and licking me in the most sensitive areas, in the most exquisite way.

I whimper and writhe beneath him. He sucks and licks harder, and the pleasure goes on and on. "Kieran, I'm still coming."

It finally ends and my body turns into a big panting mess of toneless muscle and trembling legs. "That is one good-tasting pussy you have there."

"That is one vulgar-talking mouth you have there."

He chuckles. "I could be less vulgar if you like. Maybe I could say something like madam, your vagina is an excellent vintage. Or I could say that your flower is fragrant and your nectar is sweet."

I can't do cheesy. "Go back to vulgar."

"Aye, I do vulgar well." Kieran takes his fingers out of me. "Orgasm, successful. What's next on the menu for making a baby boy?"

I push myself up and move to my knees, turning around and scooting closer to Kieran before I get on all fours. "Doggy style. It was number one on the list."

"Oh. Fuck. Yes."

I knew he was going to be keen on this one. I lower my head, pressing my forehead into the mattress, and lift my bum in the air.

"Mmm… you don't even know how many times I've fantasized about doing this to you." Kieran puts his hands on my bum and does some kind of jerking motion to make my cheeks jiggle. "Mmm… I need to get inside you before I come on the bed."

He rubs his tip through my wet center and slides into me slowly. The groan leaving his mouth can't be mistaken for anything except pure, unadulterated ecstasy. It's thrilling to hear. I want him to take great pleasure in my body, to revel being inside me on a level that he never enjoyed with any of the women who came before me.

He moves in and out, and I arch my back, tilting my bum upward until we find the perfect angle. I'm shocked by how incredible he feels in this position. "Ohhh… Kieran."

"I love hearing you say my name." He grasps my hips and squeezes, his fingertips digging into my flesh, and he uses that grip to move me on and off his cock faster. "And I love watching myself slide in and out of you."

He picks up the pace, and his legs, hips, and balls slam against my bum and thighs, making a loud slapping noise each time our bodies meet. "You hear that? That's what some good fucking sounds like."

Deep. Penetration. I understand the meaning of those two words on a whole new level now. "This feels so different." So good. I wasn't sure I would like it this way, but I do.

"I'm about to come." Kieran groans and reaches around my body. He loops his arm around my waist, pulling me hard against his body when he drives into me one last time. Balls deep. "Ohhh... fuck, Westlyn." He lies on me, his front against my back, and pins me against the bed so I can't move.

He stills and his mouth is next to my ear. "No one is ever going to take you away from me. Ever. I'll kill anyone who tries." I turn my face toward his and he leans forward, kissing the corner of my mouth roughly. "Oh fuck, I think I may be obsessed with you. The thought of losing you makes me insane."

"I'm yours, Kieran, and not because of an arrangement between our brotherhoods. I freely choose to be yours... and that can never be undone. Not by anyone."

CHAPTER SIXTEEN
WESTLYN BRECKENRIDGE

I TOLD Kieran I could go on my own to visit Mitch; it's completely safe, but he refuses to let me go without him. He's just as protective of me as Sin is of Bleu. I guess some women wouldn't like the possessiveness, but not me. I love that he's willing to do whatever it takes to keep me safe. His drive makes him an alpha, and that's a huge turn-on. A weak man would never do it for me.

He's a strong man who takes what he wants. And he wanted me. There's nothing any sexier in my eyes.

Mitch comes around his desk to hug me when Kieran and I enter his office. "Wes… what a nice surprise."

"I'm sorry to bother you. I know you must be busy, but we won't stay long."

"It's fine, but I'm curious about why you're here."

"I have an idea I'd like to discuss with you, but first I want to know what you thought of Shaw."

Mitch beams. I've never seen him smile bigger. "I think she's the most beautiful woman I've ever seen. I look forward to…" Mitch looks at Kieran and then back at me. "Coming to know her." He isn't fooling Kieran or me. We both know what he means is that he looks forward to claiming her. Knowing her as his wife.

"Shaw thinks you're handsome, which is a good start."

"Lennox didn't come out and say it, but based upon her absence at the treaty meeting, I strongly suspect that she doesn't want to marry me."

"She didn't, but her feelings have changed since meeting you." I see relief on Mitch's face. "She isn't going to come to you though."

He chuckles. "I never thought she would, but I had to give her the opportunity."

"She wants to be taken."

"That's good to know because I'm coming for her Sunday. And I told her as much." Mitch looks at Kieran. "I assume there will be no problem with that since I'm certain that you want to keep Westlyn."

I understand that Mitch's words aren't intended to be a challenge, but I don't think Kieran will feel the same. He's so hypersensitive about my being taken away from him.

"Regardless of your situation with Shaw, Westlyn stays with me. Always. I'll never give her up."

I place my hand on Kieran's leg and squeeze it to calm him. "There isn't going to be a problem. Shaw is planning to go with you, but I have an idea."

"About what?"

"She thinks it's romantic to be taken. Stolen. I was thinking that perhaps you do it before Sunday since she won't be expecting it. And I think she'll love that you couldn't wait any longer to have her."

Mitch props his elbow on the armrest of his chair and rubs his hand back and forth over his chin—he always does that when he's contemplating. "This would be all right with you and Lennox? I wouldn't want to do anything to cause problems in the treaty agreement."

Kieran places his hand on top of mine. "Westlyn thinks it's a good idea, and I'm inclined to agree. My parents do as well. And they're ready to make good on their portion of the treaty agreement."

Now for the rest of the plan. "Ellison's inception ceremony is in a few days, and there's going to be a party at Duncan's afterward. I think it's the perfect opportunity for you to take her."

"I certainly don't want to wait if I don't have to, so I like this idea."

I knew I wouldn't have to twist Mitch's arm. "Your condo isn't very romantic, and people are always coming and going. I think you should take her somewhere secluded."

"You've already chosen a place, haven't you?"

Mitch knows me well. "I have, and it's very private. The perfect place to get to know one another without interruptions." From my own experience, I've learned that interruptions aren't great.

"I say let's book it."

IT'S OFFICIAL. Ellison MacAllister is one of us. It wasn't without pain and agony on my brother's part. He still wears the proof of everything he endured for her, but Jamie has his mate. The woman he loved but thought he didn't deserve is finally his.

Duncan's is packed with Fellowship members and the Hendrys present to represent The Order. Our treaty is new, but I'm at ease just knowing that it's in place. Not that I fully trust the treaty to make the monsters of The Order behave. I have more trust that Kieran's sniping rampages have convinced them to think twice about violating the treaty or committing treason.

Kieran wraps his arms around me from behind, and I lean into him. He presses his mouth to my ear and whispers all the things he wants to do to me when we get home. He's putting our physical connection on display for all to see, and that makes me even crazier for him.

I'm falling in love with Kieran. It happens a little more every day. I wonder if people can see that when they look at me and the way I melt against him.

My heart is in this, but his is not. Kieran isn't falling in love with me. He's in lust with me. His body craves mine. Big difference. But I'll take it for now. There's always room for love to grow.

"Speech, speech, speech," the crowd chants and Jamie takes Ellison's hand to lead her onto the stage.

Ellison speaks first. "I would like to start by thanking you for coming out tonight to celebrate my inception as a Fellowship member. I'm incredibly grateful for and overwhelmed by your acceptance. I look forward to getting to know you."

Everyone cheers when she finishes, and my brother steps forward to take the spotlight. "There was a lot of interest in claiming Ellison. I feel it's necessary to make it clear where she and I stand so there's no confusion. I claimed her eleven days ago. I underwent endurance in her place three days later, hence the reason I'm limping and look like I've been hit by a train. She is mine. We have notified the district registrar of our intent to marry, and she will become my wife in eighteen days. But I left off one very important detail. I never properly asked her to be my wife."

Oh my God. He's going to properly propose, here, in front of everyone.

He drops to one knee, and Ellison covers her mouth with her hands. "Jamie."

He removes a black velvet box from the inner pocket of his jacket and cracks it open. "Ellison Brooke MacAllister. We started out as acquaintances and then friends. I felt the change happening—the one where I was falling in love with you. It was a deep, profound, true love, but I tried to fight it. Deny it. I thought I wasn't the right man for you. I was wrong. Our love was inevitable. Totally and utterly beyond our control. It knew what we needed before I did. I love you, Ellison. I want to be your husband. I want to be the father of your children. Will you marry me?"

My brother just told Ellison that he loves her in front of the entire brotherhood. I'm thrilled for them, ecstatic, but I envy the hell out of them. I want that—a man who will profess his love for me in front of his entire brotherhood.

Her smile says everything before the words come. "Yes. I will marry you."

He slides the ring on her finger and brings it to his mouth for a kiss. He lowers his voice and says something I can't hear. But I don't need to. I already know what he's saying to her. And I know what she's saying to him.

"What did they just say to each other?"

"Into me, you see."

"Is that significant?"

"Those are the most significant words one can ever speak to another. They're the definition of true intimacy, the words shared between Fellowship members when they want to express how greatly they love each other. You get to say those words to one person during your entire lifetime."

"It's the Fellowship version of mo chroí."

140

"I guess it's similar."

"I think it's the same. Mo chroí is only said during the claiming and when you express your affection to your mate. I only have one heart and if you are it, no other woman can ever be my heart. Therefore, I can never say mo chroí to any other woman."

I hadn't realized that the meaning behind *mo chroí* was so similar to *into me, you see*. I'm the only woman in Kieran's heart. I don't doubt that, but I'm not his whole heart... yet. But I'm going to be one day though.

Mitch gains my attention before walking out the front door. Our cue. He will be waiting at the back door to grab Shaw. It's my job to lure her there. "Okay, Mitch just walked out."

"I hope this doesn't backfire in our faces." Kieran still has concerns about Shaw's reaction.

"I wouldn't dare to play a part in this plan if she hadn't confessed her instant attraction to Mitch or her desire to be taken. Stop worrying, big brother. Your sister is going to be a very happy woman." Just like I was. Just like I am.

"I trust your judgment."

Shaw is suddenly wearing a frown, and I think her eyes may even be glassy. "Hey, what's wrong?"

"Mitch left. He didn't even talk to me."

She's disappointed. That's a good sign. "I thought he was interested when we spoke a few days ago. He couldn't stop looking at me or touching my hand. Was I wrong? Is that not a sign of interest?"

"I don't think you were wrong. Mitch is on the council; he's important. Probably just had to step out to handle some Fellowship duties. I wouldn't worry if I were you. He's already told you that he's coming for you on Sunday." I loop my arm through hers. "Let's go to the stockroom and sneak a drink away from everyone else. I know where they keep the good stuff."

"Lead the way." My arm is still looped through hers as we walk to the back of the pub. "Your brother really loves Ellison. It's crystal clear."

"He does, with all of his heart."

"That's what I wanted. What I was fighting so hard for. To be with a man who loves me with all of his heart." I hear sadness in Shaw's voice. Regret.

"You can have that with Mitch. Maybe not today, but it can happen."

"We didn't choose each other."

"Kieran and I didn't choose each other either, but I already feel things happening between us."

"My brother is different with you. Softer. Not the jackass he usually is with a woman, and I can't believe it. I didn't think it was possible, but things are working out between you. I see it happening right before my eyes."

I release Shaw's arm and open the back door.

"They keep the good stuff out here?"

Mitch comes out of the shadow and pulls Shaw against him, his arm around her lower back. "Yes, the best stuff." His mouth comes down on hers before she can protest. She struggles against him for a moment and then gives in, her hands diving into the back of his hair.

I think I should leave.

Mitch stops kissing her and grasps her chin. "I'm here to take what's mine, and you're not going to tell me that I can't. I've decided I want you now, and I'm not waiting anymore." He hoists Shaw over his shoulder and carries her toward the black sedan waiting behind Duncan's. She lifts her head and looks at me, smiling, and I know this was the right decision.

My plan is a success. "Have fun."

I'm on my way back into the pub when I run into Lorna and Bleu in the hallway. It's evident that Lorna's been crying. "Hey, what's going on?" Bleu motions for me to follow them into the stockroom. "Did Leith do something to her?" I will kill him if he has said something stupid like last time.

"He hasn't done anything. I'm just upset because I haven't been back to Duncan's since that day."

That day. We all know *that day* refers to when Leith humiliated Lorna and broke her heart. That was over a year ago, and she's still suffering. But Leith is too... which serves him right for everything he's done to my friend.

"Do you need to go?"

"Ellison has become one of my best friends. I hate to not be here to celebrate her inception, but this place still hurts. Seeing him still hurts. I don't think I can stay."

"If you can't, you can't. Ellison will understand. We all will." This place holds a lot of good memories and a lot of terrible ones.

Bleu wipes the falling tears from Lorna's face. "I can call Sterling to come by and take you home."

Lorna shakes her head. "Thanks, but I drove my car."

I wrap my arms around my friend and caress her hair. I feel terrible for her and maybe a little guilty for not checking in on her lately. "I'm so sorry you're hurting, Lolo."

"I got myself into this. I deserve everything that happens to me after what I did." Lorna is a self-loather who can't forgive herself. She believes she's a horrible person when that isn't the case at all.

"Don't say that."

Lorna looks at Bleu. "I still don't understand how you can be so kind to me. You or Ellison."

"How many times must I tell you that it happened before Ellison or I came along. We can't hate you for something you did with Sin and Jamie before we knew you or them."

The door opens, and Leith stands in the doorway looking at us. "What's going on in here?"

I'm certain that Lorna won't want him to know that she's in the stock-room crying over him, so I grab a bottle of whisky from the shelf. "Lorna was showing us where you keep the good stuff." She used to be head barmaid here. That sounds like a good excuse for being in the stockroom, right?

"That's not the good stuff."

Shite. "Well, you walked in before she could show us."

Lorna walks to the door and tries to push past Leith. "You can show them; I was just leaving."

Leith grasps her wrist, and she stills. He leans close. His voice is barely more than a whisper, but I'm able to make out his words. "Please don't go."

She won't even look at him. "I have to."

Bleu and I are intruding on this moment that should be private

---

between the two of them, but we have no way of getting out of the room without going through the doorway where they're standing.

Bleu moves toward the door and grabs Leith and Lorna by the wrists, pulling them into the stockroom and clearing a path for us to exit. "We're leaving, so the two of you can talk."

Lorna shakes her head. "No need. There's nothing to talk about."

Leith grasps her upper arms. "How long are you going to punish me?"

"I'm not having this conversation."

Bleu and I bolt for the door and close it once we're on the other side, leaving Lorna trapped with Leith. "I hope he pins her down and forces her to talk about what happened." I'm tempted to grab the knob and hold it since it's her only escape.

"Maybe he'll pin her down and do more than have a conversation. Some angry sex would do both of them a world of good."

Angry sex. I'll need to remember that one for future reference.

"I feel like we haven't seen each other in forever. How are things with Kieran?"

"Everything is really good. I'm happy, and I think we're on the road to a good marriage."

"What a wonderful happenstance."

"No one is more surprised than I am. I wanted to cut off his balls the night we met." Good thing I didn't. We need those balls.

"Sin says that he expects Kieran to get you pregnant right away. Something about sealing your bond so his claiming can't be undone." Bleu is still new to The Fellowship and learning our practices.

"There have been cases where a claiming has been undone when the unions didn't suit the brotherhood. It's rare, but it has happened. A pregnancy would end any possibility of undoing his claim on me, so yes. He is already working on putting an end to that possibility."

"It's such an archaic thing to do."

"One hundred percent." But it's only one of many archaic practices we have.

"I can't imagine how that must feel for you, but at least you weren't a virgin. I think that would have made it twice as scary."

I giggle. "It was twice as scary because I was a virgin."

Bleu's eyes widen. "What?"

"I lied by omission. All of you had these great sex stories. I just nodded and acted as though I had them too, but was keeping them to myself."

"I had no idea. You said you'd never marry a Fellowship man, so I assumed that's why you weren't concerned with remaining a virgin."

We're still standing in the hallway when Lorna rushes out of the stockroom. "Fuck… Lorna. Would you please come back?"

Lorna says nothing and continues walking, not even stopping to tell us what happened between Leith and her.

Uh-oh. That's not good.

Leith stands in the hallway, holding the top of his head, watching Lorna leave. "Fuck, fuck, fuck." Those are the only words he says before grabbing a bottle of whisky out of the stockroom and storming toward his office.

"That clearly didn't go well."

"I'll tell Sin so he can check on him in a while. We'll make sure he gets home safely."

I hug Bleu. "I'm guessing that the Hendrys will be ready to go now that the formalities are over."

"Probably so. I would want to get out as soon as possible if I were in the middle of an Order function."

Me too. "Maybe I can come by and visit one day next week. I miss the babies."

"Do. You won't believe how much they've grown since you saw them."

"Maybe I'll bring Kieran with me so he can practice." I'd love to see how he engages with them. I don't think he's been around babies much except for his younger siblings. But I don't guess I should worry about that. Sin was never around babies either until his came along, and yet he's an excellent father.

I don't think the bond is the only reason Kieran is driven to have a baby. I think he genuinely wants a child with me.

One more week, or somewhere there about, and we'll know.

CHAPTER SEVENTEEN

KIERAN HENDRY

I DON'T like the look on Westlyn's face. Makes me wonder if something went sideways. "Mission Mitch and Shaw is accomplished?"

"Yes. And I was right. She liked him taking her away without any warning."

Thank fuck. I wasn't looking forward to fighting for Westlyn if my sister backed out on her marriage to Mitch. "Was there some kind of delay? You were gone longer than expected."

"I ran into Bleu and Lorna in the hallway on my way back. Lorna was upset, and we had to have an impromptu girls' chat."

"Everything okay?"

Westlyn shakes her head. She looks so sad. "No. Everything is not okay, and it hasn't been for a long time."

"Lorna has relationship problems?"

"*Huge* relationship problems." Westlyn looks at me for a moment before continuing. "If I tell you what's going on, you can't say anything mean about Lorna. She's one of my best friends, and I will be pissed off if you do."

I probably will judge, but I'll keep my mouth shut if I do. "I won't say anything against your friend."

"Lorna had a really great life until her parents were killed several years ago. She was an only child, completely adored by her parents, but then suddenly all of that love was taken from her when they passed. She didn't deal with the loss very well, and she made some bad decisions regarding how to feel loved again."

"I would never judge her harshly for that."

"No one would, but that's not the end of it." Westlyn sighs. "Sin,

Jamie, and Leith are best mates. They've always done everything together... and that includes Lorna."

"She was having sex with all three men?"

"Yes."

I'm not clear about what she means. "Sex with one and then there would be a lapse in time before she had sex with another? Or do you mean she let them gangbang her?"

"Sometimes it was with one, and sometimes it was... a gangbang." I hate the word gangbang, but that's exactly what Lorna allowed them to do to her. Asked them to do.

"Fuck." That is some kinky shite.

"It happened a while ago."

I figured as much since Sinclair and Bleu have been married for a while.

"My brother got out not long after it started, but Sin and Leith kept it going with her."

"I've always wondered what something like that might be like, but never enough to try it. Probably best I didn't. I've never been good at sharing. I would be terrible at orgies."

"People weren't meant to be shared that way. It causes nothing but problems."

"All this time later and it's still causing problems?"

"Big ones. So big that it's keeping two people who love each other apart."

Sin is with Bleu. Jamie is with Ellison. "Leith and Lorna?"

"Yes. Sin was a selfish prick before Bleu. He did whatever pleased him without much regard for who he hurt. He was too self-centered to see that Leith and Lorna were falling in love with each other, and he was standing in their way."

"So Leith is in love with Lorna, but he stands by and watches his best mates fuck her?" I may not be an expert on love, but that does not sound like any form of it to me.

"It's not that simple. You have to take into consideration that Sin is their leader. They don't get to tell him to fuck off and then ride into the sunset and live happily ever after."

"I don't care. There's no way I'd stand back and watch another man fuck you."

"Pretend that I'm unclaimed, we're at The Syndicate, and your uncle's oldest son wants me. You'd tell him to fuck off and he'd obey you?"

She's right, but I can't bear to admit that I wouldn't be able to keep her from him if it were his desire to have her.

"Leith and Lorna were seeing each other one-on-one without Sin. They were growing close, starting a real relationship, but all of that ended when Sin pulled Lorna into the stockroom at Duncan's one day. Leith walked in on them having sex and assumed that she'd been seeing Sin one-on-one behind his back."

I bet that stung. "I can see why he would have been done with her at that point."

"Certainly. You can't blame Leith for being hurt, but Lorna didn't choose to have a one-on-one with Sin. She felt like she couldn't refuse her leader."

"This makes me think differently of Sinclair." He sounds like a real bastard.

"Sin didn't know that Lorna wanted the gangbanging to stop but was too afraid to refuse him. And he didn't know that Lorna and Leith were in love."

"He never found out his best mate loved the girl they were fucking?"

"He eventually found out and tried to make things right by bringing Leith and Lorna back together, but it backfired in the worst way." Westlyn grimaces. "Lorna overheard Leith saying terrible things about her. Of course, he was lashing out and didn't mean any of the things he said, but it was too late. She heard him. And she can neither forgive nor forget. His words haunt her day and night."

"I think it's safe to say that those two should probably move on."

"But they can't because they're in love."

He can't forget what she did, and she can't forget what he said. "Sometimes pain that cuts that deep can't be healed."

"You sound like you know something about that?"

I hear what I think is jealousy in Westlyn's voice. "Not me. I've never been in love. It was my best mate from The Syndicate who went through a painful situation with a woman he loved."

I didn't comprehend his pain because I'd never been in love, but I'm beginning to understand his devastation.

I'm beginning to know what love feels like.

WESTLYN STANDS in the bathroom doorway looking at me, saying nothing. "What is it?"

She frowns. "I just got my period."

"Oh." I hope she doesn't feel like we've failed. "It wasn't possible for you to get pregnant then. You would have ovulated before the first time we had sex since you're getting your period today."

Her head tilts. "It's so weird that you know that. I'm a woman, and I don't even know that kind of stuff about my own body. How did you get so educated on conceiving a baby?"

I guess that kind of information does sound odd coming from me. "It's my duty to get you pregnant. My father taught me conception 101 before I claimed you."

"You don't seem disappointed that I'm not pregnant."

"I'll get to stay balls deep inside you in a couple of weeks when you are ovulating. Nothing disappointing about that, doll." That brings a smile to her beautiful face.

"I guess the upside to not being pregnant is that you get to keep trying."

"That's a very good way of looking at it." I hold out my arms for her to come to me, and I pull her onto my lap once she's within arm's reach. "I'm going to wrinkle your suit before you even get to work."

"Don't care." I wrap my arms around her and squeeze. "What time are you meeting everyone at the bridal shop?"

"Ten o'clock."

"Should be an interesting day for the bridal shop employees. Three brides. Three appointments. You're all getting married over a three-week period, and you're all related in one way or another."

"I hope none of us fall in love with the same dress. That would be a tragedy."

"I see Shaw going for a dress that makes her look like a princess. One with the big skirt on the bottom."

"That's a ball gown. Not my style and I don't think it would be Ellison's either."

Good. I'm not a fan of those kinds of dresses. "Don't choose anything too sexy or revealing. I don't want to have to kill anyone for having impure thoughts about my wife."

"But I want to look good for you."

"And you will. You'll be beautiful in whatever dress you choose, but I'd like it to cover your body. I don't want you to walk down the aisle with your tits bulging out of the top or the dress to be so tight that it shows the brothers every curve you have. Those are for my eyes only."

"I'll choose a dress that makes you proud to take me as your wife."

I bring her hand to my mouth and kiss it. "Thank you."

"I'm not looking forward to the exchange that could happen between Ellison and my mother. I hope Mum doesn't act like a total bitch."

Westlyn is heartbroken because her mother renounced her brother over his marrying Ellison. And I don't like to see my mate hurting.

"Do you think she can control herself enough to not act like a bitch?" Because from what I've seen of Torrie Breckenridge, she couldn't stop if she tried. She is what she is, through and through.

"I'm not sure, and I'm terrified that she's going to ruin this appointment for Ellison."

"Ellison is marrying your brother and is therefore an extension of our family. Don't be surprised if my mum takes a stand against Ellison being mistreated." Torrie had better mind her behavior. My mum won't hesitate to put her in her place.

"Isobel was already going to be there to support Shaw because she's marrying Mitch, but Bleu has asked her to also serve as Ellison's mother figure since their mother is dead. If Mum misbehaves, Isobel won't hesitate to slap her silly. And probably enjoy it."

"I like Isobel. I feel I owe her a debt for setting me straight about you." When I left that first treaty meeting, I was planning to force-claim Westlyn when I returned to the compound. Had zero idea that I would have been raping a virgin. I was so angry because I believed her to be a whore and would have no doubt been rough with her. I could have unknowingly injured her. All of that makes me cringe inside when I think about it now.

"She changed my mind about you as well."

I'm still wondering what might have happened between Isobel and my father. "I think Dad may have had some kind of relationship with your aunt."

"What do you mean?"

"They knew each other before they married. He looked like he'd seen a ghost when he saw Isobel at the meeting with The Fellowship council. He wouldn't stop looking at her." It made me feel weird seeing him stare at her, like it was a transgression against Mum. "And then when she got into the car with us, they both said that it was good to see each other again. And he called her Issy. I can't imagine a casual acquaintance calling her by that name."

"Isobel always hated Thane. She was in love with someone else when she was forced to marry him. She always blamed Thane for causing her to lose the love of her life. I wonder if that man was Lennox."

"I think it could be. And that could make for an awkward situation at the bridal shop if my mother knows they had a relationship." I think my mum and dad tell each other everything, so I'm certain she would know.

"If they did, it was over a long time ago. And we know that your father has been loyal to your mum. I think it'll be fine."

"I agree. My mum has been married to my dad for twenty-nine years, and they have five children together. She isn't going to be upset over a fling that might have happened before they married."

"Have you had any flings that I should know about? Any relationships that were more than just sex?"

"No."

"You've never loved a woman?"

"Never." But I think I may be beginning to.

CHAPTER EIGHTEEN

WESTLYN BRECKENRIDGE

IT'S DONE. Ellison and Jamie are man and wife. I'm thrilled for them... but disheartened for myself.

I will marry Kieran Hendry a week from today, but I won't see adoration in his eyes as I walk down the aisle. His face won't alight with pure love and reverence as he makes me his wife.

And that's what I want. His love.

I've fallen for the man who claimed me as his own. My mate. My husband. What a fortunate circumstance that should be, but it's not. Not when my love is unrequited.

I'm staring out the window, watching the streetlights zoom by, when Kieran reaches for my hand. "What's wrong, doll?"

"Nothing."

"We don't lie to each other."

How do I tell Kieran the truth? That I love him and want his love in return when I'm not even sure that he's the loving kind.

"Tell me what's bothering you."

"Seeing Ellison and Jamie together tonight made me see what I won't have on my wedding day."

"Tell me what it is, and I'll get it for you."

I hesitate, biting my lip, gathering my courage to say the words. "A husband who loves me."

I've knocked Kieran for a loop. How do I know that? Because he doesn't reply. Not a single word. I turn to stare out the window again, disappointed when I see that he's not even going to try to pacify me with pretty words.

It's late and I'm exhausted by the time we return to the compound.

Things between us are awkward, and neither of us say a word as we go inside. Still no words while we fall into our bedtime routine.

I'm wearing one of my long gowns, and as usual, Kieran isn't wearing a stitch when he gets in bed beside me. We've had sex every single night since he claimed me, except for the days I had my period. I wonder if he believes that he's entitled to sex tonight.

He's not.

I turn off the light and lie on my side, my back to him. I don't say a word. I'm afraid I'll burst into tears... and I would hate that. Hate for him to see me being weak... because he doesn't love me.

I feel the wetness collecting in my eyes. I squeeze my lids tightly, hoping to stop it, but it only makes the tears fall down my face. Dammit. Kieran has never seen me cry, and I don't want him to now either.

I'm not that girl... the one who is weak and whiny and weepy.

He turns off his bedside lamp, and we lie in the darkness. More silence, except for our breathing and my occasional sniffle.

At least ten minutes have passed when Kieran says, "I feel more for you than I've ever felt for any woman."

Maybe that's supposed to make me happy, but it doesn't "How many women have you ever been in love with?" I already know the answer.

"None."

"You've never felt anything for a woman, but with me you feel *more... than... nothing*. Wow. That makes me get all kinds of butterflies in my stomach." I wish he hadn't said anything at all.

"I didn't say that I feel *more than nothing* for you. Those are your words."

"Doesn't matter."

"It does matter. It matters very much because you're unhappy. I don't want you to ever be unhappy, not even for a second." He moves closer and wraps his arm around my waist. Nothing sexual. Just an affectionate embrace. "I'm falling for you, doll. I feel it happening more and more every day."

"Are you?" I hate the desperate hopefulness I hear in my own voice. I sound pathetic.

"I am." He snuggles closer. "Love is like a rose. It blooms at the perfect time when it's at its most beautiful but only after being nurtured.

That's what our relationship needs: to be nurtured so it can bloom when it's at its most beautiful."

You don't expect poetic words like those to come from the mouth of a killer. "That's a good way of putting it."

"Do you love me, Westlyn?"

Surely he knows that I do. I wouldn't bring this up if I didn't. He says that he's falling for me. That's different from loving me, and it's not fair for him to ask me to declare my love for him. "You don't get to ask me that."

"I do get to ask you that. Tell me. Do you love me?"

I could lie and say no. I could refuse to answer one way or the other. But what's the point? "Yes."

"Say it."

"No." It's cruel of him to ask that of me when he can't say it back.

He turns on the lamp, pushes me to my back and gets on top of me, his eyes staring directly at mine. "I want to hear you say it."

I close my eyes, press my lips together, and shake my head. Defying him. "I won't give you that satisfaction until you're able to say the words in return."

He lowers his forehead to mine. "Please, Westlyn. I can't recall in twenty-eight years ever hearing those words said to me. You'd be the first to say them."

We are so much alike, he and I. Both of us yearning to be loved.

It's a pain I know all too well. Kieran doesn't know that I've never been told those words either, or how desperately I too want to hear them. I understand his deep pain, and that is why I can't withhold those words from him although I already know I won't hear them in return.

I open my eyes and look at those dark orbs staring at me. They're black like his heart and soul, but I want to be his light so that he doesn't have to remain alone in the dark. "I love you."

He closes his eyes for a moment and then opens them. "Say it again. Please. With my name."

"I love you, Kieran."

"Those words… they do something to me, Westlyn. I can't begin to explain it." He closes his eyes and softly presses a kiss to my mouth. "Things are changing between us. Growing… *blooming*. We're becoming so much more than two people who are marrying to bring peace to our brotherhoods."

It's not an *I love you*, but I'll take it.

For now.

He deepens our kiss and gently rocks against me. "I want to make love to you. No fucking. No trying to make a baby. Just you and me connecting. Getting closer."

Well, withholding sex from him tonight is out of the question now. Who could say no to that? Not this girl.

I wrap my arms around his shoulders and nod. "Make love to me."

I STAND on the platform in the bridal shop for my final fitting before I marry Kieran in three days. I can't believe it's been almost a full month since a hood was placed over my head, and I was tossed into the back of a limo to kneel before him. *My master.* That's what he called himself. And to some degree he is, because he certainly does own me.

Mo chroí. That's what he is. My heart.

"Looks like a perfect fit," Isobel says. I asked her to come with me today because I'm angry with my mother and humiliated by her behavior. I've personally witnessed her being inappropriate toward Lennox, and I strongly suspect she may have made a pass at him in private. I don't think he would take her up on her offer. Kieran assures me that people from The Syndicate are faithful to their mates. No exceptions.

He is a handsome man, but he's married to Arabella. She has no right to proposition him. There are plenty of men within The Fellowship who don't have wives. But that's not what my mother would want. She's hungry for power and position, and Lennox has plenty of that.

This is the first time I've been alone with Isobel since Kieran and I discussed her having a past relationship with his father. I wonder if I'd offend her by asking about it. "Kieran says that you and Lennox know each other."

"We did a long time ago."

Arabella didn't act strangely toward Isobel, but it's possible she doesn't know about their prior relationship. "Is Lennox the man you were in love with before you married Thane?"

"Ye know about that, huh?" Isobel grins. "Lennox's older brother, William, and I were in love." William will be the leader of The Syndicate after Douglas Hendry dies. "My father thought a match with Thane was more beneficial. I was heartbroken. I spent a lot of years blaming Thane, and eventually he came tae hate me as much as I hated him. Oor relationship, however, has improved over the last year. We tolerate one another, and sometimes we're even cordial."

I've seen a change in their relationship. They do seem to tolerate one another more. I think sharing grandchildren has helped to soften them toward each other.

"William will be at my wedding." With his wife.

"Yes, he will."

"Have you seen him since you were married off to Thane?"

"No."

"Do you still love him?"

"I will always love William, but that doesnae matter. I'm married. He's married… and people from The Syndicate don't stray. Not even those in leadership roles." Isobel forces a smile and holds out my veil. "I want tae see ye in this too."

The bridal shop attendant sees us struggling with the placement. "Let me help you with that." Feels like she places at least a dozen pins in my hair. Totally unnecessary; I'm only trying it on.

"You look beautiful. You're going to take Kieran's breath away."

I hope he doesn't think it's too sexy.

"Delivery for Miss Breckenridge," a man says as he walks toward me carrying a large bouquet of flowers. It's odd that I would have a delivery to the bridal shop. Must be from Kieran since he's the only one who knows I'm here right now.

Isobel cuts off the man. "I'll take those. Dinnae want her to soil her wedding dress. She's getting married in three days."

"No, she isn't." The man shoves the flowers at Isobel, knocking her to the floor, and the seamstress screams and backs away from me. He rushes at me with a raised knife, and I lift my arms to shield myself. I instantly feel the sharp burn of his knife slicing through my flesh. Feels like a nightmare happening in slow motion.

White. Red. Black.

It happens in that order.

The *white* wedding dress saturated with *red* blood and *black* taking over my vision.

CHAPTER NINETEEN

KIERAN HENDRY

I'M LOOKING at The Order's ledgers, and the shite doesn't add up. I strongly suspect that someone is skimming off the top. Wouldn't be the first time that has ever been done. Also wouldn't be the first time I've been asked to step in and rid the brotherhood of a thief.

Why can't these fucking people just do what they're supposed to do with honor? It would make my job so much easier.

My father appears in the doorway of my office. "Son, you need to get your M24."

I don't question. I just react by going to the gun cabinet and removing the case that houses my favorite sniper. "Only the M24?"

"Take the Magnums too. I'm not sure what we're dealing with yet."

He comes to my gun cabinet, and I pass the Magnum cases to him. "What do you think has happened?"

"We'll talk about it after we get going."

My father doesn't give me time to ask any questions once we're in the car. "Load now. We'll talk after you finish."

Shite. That's weird. He always briefs me while I prepare.

"Yes, sir." I finish with the last Magnum and place it on the seat. "What's going on?"

My father hesitates, and that's when I know something bad has happened. Something personal. Something that involves me. "A man came into the bridal shop and attacked Westlyn."

I'm not a man who is easily frightened, but I'm fucking terrified right now. "Is she…" Alive? I can't bring myself to say that word.

"She made it through."

I bring the coiled side of my fist to my mouth. I cough, trying to clear the lump I feel there, but it doesn't move. My voice breaks when I ask, "What did he do to her?"

"I don't know the details. Only that he used a knife."

He cut my doll. "Where is she?"

"The Fellowship Infirmary. Jamie and Ellison are treating her wounds."

I'm sure Jamie is an excellent doctor, and I'm certain he'll only give the best care to his sister. I'm grateful for that.

"I wish I knew more, but Isobel was very distraught when she called, and the conversation was very short."

My father and I don't speak further during the remainder of the drive to The Fellowship Infirmary, and the silence feeds my fear. The limo barely stops before I'm out of the car and running toward the house that The Fellowship has transformed into a place to treat their wounded.

Isobel is holding the front door open for me. "She's in the acute trauma room. First door on the left." I stop at the door before entering and inhale deeply, preparing myself for the worst.

Westlyn is lying on her back, her eyes closed. Her skin is as pale as the wedding gown and veil she's still wearing, both saturated with red stains. There are two squares of white gauze taped on her face, one covering her chin and the other covering her left cheek. Blood has seeped through the center of both.

I walk around the stretcher and stand next to her. I want to take her hand in mine, but I can't because Jamie is sewing on her lower arm. "How bad is it?"

"She has numerous defensive lacerations on her lower arms and hands, a few on her chest and breasts, and then those two on her face. She's going to need a lot of sutures. We'll be working on her for a while."

I watch Jamie insert a suture needle into her skin, and she doesn't flinch. "Is she sedated?"

"Aye, and I'm using local anesthesia. She was in a lot of pain and couldn't be still. I need her to be relaxed while I do this so that the edges of the lacerations will come together smoothly. If she's tense, they'll be jagged and cause puckering in the skin when they heal. I'm suturing as many as I can from the inside, and we'll close the skin with surgical glue to reduce scarring."

"Did she tell you that she could be pregnant?"

Jamie stops and looks up at me. "She didn't say anything about that."

"We've been trying. It would be very early if she were, but I assume that's something you'd need to know before giving her certain drugs."

"What she's had so far is fine, but we'll double check any further medications before giving them to her to be sure they're safe during pregnancy."

Jamie returns to suturing, and I kneel next to Westlyn. I lean forward and press my forehead to the side of her head so my mouth is over her ear. "I'm so sorry this happened to you." I caress the top of her veiled hair. "You're going to be just fine, doll. Jamie and Ellison are taking good care of you."

"Do you know who did this to my sister?" I can tell that Jamie is working hard to choke back his emotion.

"Not yet, but I am going to find out."

"What do you plan to do to him?"

A snipe is too good for whoever did this. "He's going to eat the barrel of my Magnum, but not before I make him sorry that he came after my mate."

"I want him to suffer for this."

Isobel is standing in the doorway. "I hit him hard with the heavy end of a crystal vase. He has a severe laceration tae the back of his head. I know because he was bleeding profusely."

I hope he doesn't die of a head injury before I get to him.

Jamie looks up at me. "Probably has a concussion and will need to be seen by an emergency doctor. I have connections at Royal Infirmary. I can find out who comes in with a head trauma."

"In the meantime, I will have my brothers do a head check of all Order men to clear them." I believe we have them under control, but this is similar to something one of them would do. "It sounds like you saved her, Isobel. Thank you for being there with her." Her mother would have probably stood back and done nothing.

Isobel looks over at Westlyn. "She fought valiantly and used the defense skills Bleu taught her. I dinnae think she'd have survived that attack otherwise. That man was determined to kill her."

Westlyn moans. "Kier... an," she whispers.

"I'm right here, doll."

Her eyes are slits and her pupils look out of focus. "Can't see me... in my wedding... dress. Bad luck."

"Don't worry about that for even a second." I stand and lean over her so that I can see her eyes. "Can you hear what I'm saying?"

"Yes."

"Mo chroí. That's what you are to me. My heart. And I love you. I. Love. You. Don't doubt that for a second."

"Mo... chroí... love... you... too."

Her eyes close and her breathing becomes deep and steady again. I highly doubt that she'll remember me saying those words to her, but she won't have to. I'm going to tell her so much that she'll doubt my sanity.

"Adjust the light for me, Mac." Ellison grabs the handle of the overhead light and points it at the inside of Westlyn's arm. "And I need you to open her sleeves all the way up."

Ellison picks up the big scissors and cuts up the center of the wedding gown's sleeve until she reaches Westlyn's shoulder. "She loved this dress so much."

"It's exactly what I imagined her wearing." And what I would have picked for her. Beautiful and chaste.

"She chose it because of the sleeves and higher neckline; she said that you didn't want her to wear anything revealing."

She listened and chose this dress to please me. "Can't lie. I've become a jealous man where she's concerned. I didn't want other men looking at my mate with impure thoughts."

"Your jealousy probably saved her life. The thick lace on these sleeves prevented the knife from slicing deeper."

Thane comes into the trauma room. He looks at Westlyn and grimaces. "How bad?"

"There'll be some mild scarring, but she'll make a full recovery," Jamie says.

Angry eyes shift to me. "You and Lennox told us that you would get The Order under control. You said that we would no longer have to worry about them attacking our women, and now my niece is lying here butchered like a piece of meat."

Thane is furious, and we are too, but he's fingering the wrong people.

"We've gone to great extreme to show them what happens to brothers who choose to go against us. We have them under control. Trust me. They didn't do this."

"I disagree. You don't know them the way we do. This is just like them to attack one of our women unexpectedly."

"The attack is very Order-like. I'm not saying that it isn't, but Westlyn is no longer one of your women. She's mine, and that makes her one of our women."

"Not yet. I can't let you marry her if she's going to be in danger."

Oh, fuck no. We made an agreement, and I'll go to war with the whole brotherhood if need be. He isn't taking her from me.

"She's my mate. I've claimed her."

"The claiming can be undone under these kinds of circumstances."

"Not if she's pregnant."

"Is she pregnant?"

"It's very possible. We've been trying." Every single day.

Thane looks at Jamie. "Test her."

She hasn't even had time to miss her period yet. "Would a pregnancy test turn positive if she's very early pregnant?"

"Depends on how early, but probably not unless we do a blood test. I don't keep any kind of pregnancy tests, urine or blood, at the infirmary."

Thane clearly doesn't care for that answer. "The only way you'll marry my niece is if you've already gotten your seed into her."

"Or if I prove it wasn't an Order member who did this."

He points his finger at me where I'm kneeling behind Westlyn, trying to intimidate me. But I'm not. "Concrete proof. That's what it'll take for me to go along with your marriage to her."

"I'll get the proof," I call out to him as he goes out the door.

Thane is right about one thing. If The Order did this then we don't have the control we thought we had. If that's the case, I don't deserve to have Westlyn as my wife if I can't protect her from my own people.

Jamie finishes with her left arm and moves to start on the right. "You must love hearing that there's a possibility that I won't marry your sister."

"You love my sister, and she loves you. I see it with my own eyes and hear it in the words you exchange with one another. She'll be heartbroken if she can't marry you. So no, I don't love hearing that there's a possibility you won't be her husband."

"Your impression of me has changed?"

"I still think you're a dick for threatening to beat and rape Westlyn and Ellison. And for taunting me when you knew I was scared out of my fucking mind for both of them. But I'm grateful you didn't harm either. I know how loving you are to my sister, and that means a lot." He holds out his hand to Ellison for a new suture. "And just so you know, I'm still pissed off at you for shooting me."

"Sorry about shooting you. I didn't want to do it, but you were going to thwart my plan for taking Westlyn."

"Ah, fuck. It all worked out."

"Until now." I stroke Westlyn's hair. "I can't lose her." I love her too much.

Westlyn goes through cycles of wake and sleep while Jamie and Ellison tend her wounds. Every time she wakes, I tell her how much I love her, and she tells me the same. The sewing goes on for hours. I know Jamie is taking great care in suturing her to the best of his ability so she'll be left with as minimal scarring as possible.

It's late afternoon by the time all of Westlyn's wounds are closed. The more agony I see her in, the more my fury multiplies. "Will you give her something to make her sleep?" I don't want her to remember any of this pain.

Ellison strokes the top of her head. "We'll make sure she rests well."

"I don't want her to wake and find me gone, but I have to go figure out who's responsible for this attack."

"It's okay, Kieran. She shouldn't wake anytime soon, but if she does, we'll tell her where you are and what you're doing," Ellison says.

"Please don't tell her what Thane said." I don't want her to be upset on top of this.

"Won't say a word."

"Can you call your contact at the Royal Infirmary before I leave? I'd like to know if the motherfucker showed up there before I go to the trouble of investigating every Order member."

"Sure."

Jamie and Ellison both step out, and I'm alone with Westlyn for the first time. I take this private moment to look at her wounds. There are so many slashes on her skin that she looks like she ran through a plate-glass window. "I'm so sorry this happened to you, doll. But I'm going to find the fucker who did this to you. And when I do, I'm going to make him sorry."

Jamie returns. "I can't fucking believe it. There was a man who came in with a blunt force trauma to the skull a few hours ago. He has a concussion and is being kept for observation."

"Sounds like that could be our man. Is Isobel still here?"

"I'll get her," Ellison says.

Isobel comes into the trauma room. "Jamie says the man who did this may be at Royal Infirmary. I need you to go with me and identify him."

"Of course. That animal needs tae be put down."

"Did you get a name?"

"Tavis Ewart," Jamie says.

"Ewart," Isobel says. "That name is very familiar tae me."

"I'm still not familiar with every brother, but I don't recall one being named Tavis Ewart on the list of Order members." I drop a text to my dad, telling him to check the roll for this asshole's name.

"Feels like I've known an Ewart before, but I can't put my finger on it right now."

"Maybe it'll come back to you when you get a better look at his face."

"Maybe."

"Tavis Ewart's room, please."

The woman keys in his name and frowns. "Looks like Mr. Ewart was discharged."

Fuck. "How long ago?"

"I'm sorry. I can't give you that information."

Isobel and I walk away from the clerk's desk. "What are we going tae do now?"

"Only thing I can do. My brother is going to hack into the system and get his home address." Let's hope he's forgiven me for choking him.

"Yer brother's contribution is hacking?"

"Yes, ma'am."

"We dinnae have a hacker, but times are changing. We need one."

"Yes, ma'am, every brotherhood needs a hacker." Don't know what we'd do without Maddock.

I phone Maddock and put him to work on locating Tavis Ewart. He's fast as fuck. Has a home address for me in under five minutes. "Looks like we're going to a village on the outer edges of Edinburgh."

The farther we drive, the more convinced I become that Tavis Ewart is not Order. None of our members live on this side of the city. It's a dump.

"I've been over this way before."

"What circumstances would bring a leader's wife to find herself in this slum?"

"I came with my daughter-in-law. We were investigating a lead aboot Abram." The car stops in front of a stone cottage. "His lover lives here. Cameron…" Isobel's eyes widen. "Cameron Ewart. That's no coincidence."

I'm confident that we've found the man who attacked Westlyn. I just don't know why. "A man who lives in the same household as Abram's lover attacked his daughter more than a year after Abram's death. What does that mean?"

"I have no idea, but we are about to find out."

The door is unlocked, so I walk in as though I've been invited. "Who the hell are you?"

"Is this him?"

Isobel answers without hesitation. "That's definitely him."

"Are you the police? Are you arresting me?"

"You're going to wish I were the police."

"Who are you?"

"I'm the man who's going to make you sorry that you attacked my fiancée with a knife."

"Is the Breckenridge girl dead?" His voice is so cold.

"No." I see his disappointment. "She didn't do anything to you. Why did you try to kill her?"

"I want to see Abram."

He doesn't know that Abram's dead? "Oh, you're going to see Abram all right... in hell."

"What does that mean?"

"Abram is dead."

"You're lying to protect him."

"Abram has been dead for a while."

"So has my little girl."

"Cameron?" Isobel says.

"Yes. How do you know her name?"

"Abram used tae come here tae..." Isobel pauses. "Spend time with Cameron. She had information aboot him that I needed, and I spoke to her."

"Did you know that she was dead?"

"I did not. I never saw her again after that day we spoke. I'm sorry tae hear that."

The bastard wails. "Abram killed her."

"How?" Isobel says.

"The doctors told me that she had been choked. She didn't die right away. She was in a coma for almost a year before I lost her. And that bastard did it. He killed my little girl."

I'm not going to ask how he knows it was Abram because I'm sure he's probably right.

"I'm sorry for your loss, but you're coming with us. You have a mess to clear up for me."

"What kind of mess?"

"Don't worry about it right now. Either walk out on your own or have both of your kneecaps shot off and be carried out of here. Your choice."

He chooses to walk.

Isobel and I take Tavis Ewart to one of The Fellowship's warehouses. This isn't The Order's mess. I'm not killing this man on our territory. This is Abram's doings, and The Fellowship will be responsible for the cleanup.

My father and brothers are the first to arrive. As far as I know, it's the first time Isobel has seen my father since the night I kidnapped Westlyn.

Dad isn't pleased to see Isobel here. "Issy shouldn't be here for this."

Isobel is a fiery redhead. My father should know better than to talk to me about her as though she isn't standing there. "This man attacked Westlyn in front of me. I want tae be here. I hope ye aren't under the impression that I'm too soft for this because ye'd be wrong."

"I know you're tough, but this isn't a place for a lady."

They spar back and forth about her being here, like old friends, but then the conversation takes a different turn. "Aren't you going to ask me about William?"

"Wasn't planning tae. No good can come from it," she says.

"He asked about you."

Isobel's full attention has been captured. "What did he want tae know aboot me?"

"If you looked the same. If you are happy. If you had asked about him."

"I…"

Their conversation is cut short when Thane, Sin, and Mitch arrive. I requested the entire council be present with the exception of Jamie because I need all of them to be clear about where the fault lies regarding Westlyn's attack. I also need them to witness with their own eyes to what degree I'm willing to go to avenge this attack on my mate. "Meet Tavis Ewart."

"One of your Order members?" Thane says.

I punch Tavis. "Tell him who you are and how your life came to be intertwined with Westlyn's."

"Abram killed my daughter, so I came to kill his. But this guy told me that she didn't die, and that means I can't be charged with murder."

Poor bastard doesn't know that I am his judge and jury. "You attempted to murder my mate, and the punishment is the same."

"I'll get a lawyer. I'll never do time."

"You are correct, Mr. Ewart. You won't serve a single day in prison." I'm itching to take out my Magnum, but I hold steady in case Thane has questions for this man. "As you can see, Tavis Ewart is not a member of The Order. Westlyn's attack was an extension of a murder that Abram committed. My people did not do this to her. Are you satisfied with this as proof, or do you want to question him further?"

"You aren't a member of The Order?"

"Is that some kind of cult or something?"

Thane flicks his hand. "He's not Order."

"Do you withdraw your objection to my marriage to Westlyn?"

"I withdraw my objection... and request pardon." A pardon. Not something a leader ever has to ask for, but he did nonetheless.

I nod. "Pardon granted."

"What the fuck kind of rubbish are you people talking?"

I choose to forgo torture because the man lost his daughter. He has suffered enough at the hands of Abram Breckenridge.

I place my Magnum at the back of his head and pull the trigger. Only one shot is needed when it's coming from one of the most powerful handguns in production.

"Fuck... fuuuck." Mitch's eyes are huge. "You blew off half of his head."

I don't think my new brother-in-law is accustomed to being on this side of business. "This is what happens to anyone who dares to harm Westlyn. I will never hesitate to kill for her... because she is my heart, and I love her."

I might as well confess who and what I am since we are going to be allies. "This is what I do. I am an assassin. The best you'll ever meet. We are now allies, but more importantly, we are family. If you need my services, you need only just ask."

Thane offers his hand. "Our alliance is in good standing. Just have to get Westlyn and you married."

I want that more than anything.

CHAPTER TWENTY
WESTLYN BRECKENRIDGE

THE LACE SLEEVES on my new wedding dress are long and come down into a V. They conceal the pink lines all over my lower arms and hands. The neckline is slightly off the shoulder, but it covers the healing slashes on my chest. The ones on my face, those can't be hidden. Only camouflaged with cosmetics.

Kieran says that he doesn't see my scars. I know he does; he gives himself away because he kisses them often.

Jamie says I'm healing well, and with more time he expects minimal scarring for most of the wounds. I hope he's right. I want as few reminders of the attack as possible. I want to put it behind me and move on with my life. My life with Kieran as my husband.

We were forced to postpone the wedding longer than either of us wanted. Recovery has been harder than expected because so many of my wounds are located in areas where my skin must stretch to accommodate movement. It's been some agonizing months. Agonizing because of the pain, but also agonizing because I want so desperately to be married to Kieran. Today, we finally become husband and wife.

"The zipper isn't cooperating. You're going to have to suck in."

"Easier said than done." My belly has had a growth spurt since my final dress fitting. It's like I went to bed with a flat stomach and woke up with a bump.

"She's already getting fat." It's just like my mother to say something like that.

"She's not fat. Her body is expanding to accommodate the bairn inside her," Isobel says.

I might be self-conscious about the way my body is expanding if Kieran didn't constantly tell me how beautiful I look with his child inside me. I thought he was insatiable before, but he can't keep his hands off me and my growing belly.

Lorna pulls harder on the zipper and I feel the dress suddenly become tight around my waist. "Got it."

"Mmm... that is tight. I hope I make it through the ceremony and reception without busting the seams." The seamstress expanded it as much as she could. There's not a lot of fabric inside the seams holding this dress together.

Bleu studies my waist. "Are you sure you don't have twins? That's exactly what my belly did when I was pregnant with the boys."

I place my hand over my bump. "Doctor says there's only one in here."

"And let's all pray that it's a boy." My mother wants the bragging rights of calling herself the grandmother of the next leader.

I know Kieran would love to have a son. I would too, but now that I'm pregnant, he also says that he'd love to have a little girl with my hair and eyes. "Kieran and I will be happy with whatever we get. We're far more concerned with our child being born healthy."

I was barely pregnant when I was attacked. I know that the baby wasn't injured, but I've taken so many drugs the last several months. Jamie says they're all safe for the baby, but I always have that fear in the back of my mind... that maybe I harmed my own child by taking medicine for pain when I should have suffered through it.

"Kieran may say that he'll be happy with whatever you get, but he wants a boy. Trust me. They all do. Your father wanted all boys. He was very angry that you and Evanna were girls."

What a shitty thing to say to your daughter—even if it is the truth—on her wedding day. I might be hurt if I didn't know that my father was an evil bastard.

"Stop talking, Torrie." Isobel warns. "Ye've not said anything positive the entire day, so shut yer gob."

"Westlyn doesn't know how men are. I'm just telling her how her husband really feels."

"Say another word and I'll slap ye so hard that yer ears ring. And it won't be church bells ye're hearing." Isobel isn't kidding. She'll do it. She's done it before.

"Maybe she'll renounce you too, so you don't have to listen to her bullshit anymore," Evanna whispers.

"I wish." But there's no way my mother would renounce me. I'm marrying a leader. Her new son-in-law has too much money and power for her to walk away from me.

My mother renounced Jamie for marrying Ellison. She renounced Evanna for being in love with a cleaner—a brother who cleans up the bloody mess and bodies following a kill. Mother says that Craig is the lowest of the low and beneath Evanna's status. But Evanna has chosen him; she loves him. He has claimed her, and they are going to be married at the end of the month.

I'm proud of my sister. She's no longer allowing Mum to control her.

Isobel places her hand on my arm. "It's almost time. We should probably go."

I look at my reflection one last time. Not much longer as Westlyn Breckenridge. I'll be Mrs. Kieran Bryce Hendry the next time I look at myself in the mirror. "I'm ready."

CHAPTER TWENTY-ONE

KIERAN HENDRY

I'M STANDING in the center of a stone arch between two large round pillars in St. Giles Cathedral, waiting for my beloved. It's an unusually sunny day. Rays of sunlight passing through the stained-glass windows look like modern-day graffiti on the centuries-old stone surrounding us.

The bridal chorus begins, and Thane and Westlyn enter the cathedral. They must walk from my left to reach the center aisle. Thane's body is blocking my view of Westlyn, but then they reach the aisle and turn to face me, giving me my first look at my bride.

And I can't take my eyes off of her.

She's so beautiful, it takes my breath away.

People use that expression all the time. I thought it was just a saying, but it's a real thing, and this moment is proof of it. My face and hands are tingling. My heart is beating so fast that it can't carry oxygen to my brain fast enough to keep up with the sudden demand.

Westlyn's arm is looped through Thane's, and they begin their walk toward us. I had no idea what her dress and veil would look like this time or how she would wear her hair, but everything about her is perfection. Slightly off-white in color. A strapless dress with a lace overlay, her shoulders peeking out at the top. Her body is covered so she appears chaste, but she's showing just enough skin to be sexy. Gorgeous.

She smiles, and her eyes never leave mine as she approaches. Thane shakes my hand and kisses Westlyn's cheek before placing her hand in mine.

She turns and passes her bouquet of white roses to Evanna and then places both hands in mine. I slowly rub my thumbs back and forth over the top of her hands, hearing little of what the minister is saying.

Our ceremony is traditional. Music. Vows. Ring exchange. We're saving our true vows for the reception.

The minster rambles on for too long as I anxiously wait to hear him tell me to kiss my bride. When he finally does, I lean close and cradle her face. "Mo chroí."

"Mo chroí."

I press a soft, loving kiss against her lips. Nothing too passionate. I'm saving that for later when we're alone.

"I now present to you, Mr. and Mrs. Kieran Bryce Hendry."

A LARGE WHITE tent stands in the backyard of our compound. It covers tables adorned in white cloth with glowing candles and huge floral arrangements. Several crystal chandeliers hang from the ceiling, making this outdoor room feel elegant, courtesy of the event planning done by Isobel and my mother... and *overseen* by Torrie. Which means Isobel and my mum did all of the work.

My father has Westlyn and I join him on a raised platform in front of all of the guests—members of The Syndicate, The Fellowship, and The Order. There are hundreds of people in attendance. "We gather here tonight to celebrate the marriage of my eldest son, Kieran Bryce Hendry of The Order, formerly of The Syndicate, to Westlyn Leigh Breckenridge Hendry of The Fellowship. We are also celebrating the inception of Westlyn into The Order as one of our own."

My wife and I approach the small table adorned to match the larger tables throughout with one exception—a dagger. The bleeding ceremony is traditional. It can't be skipped, but I've dreaded doing this—slicing Westlyn's skin so we can bleed together.

"Kieran Bryce Hendry, do you accept responsibility for Westlyn Leigh Breckenridge Hendry?"

"I do."

"Take the dagger."

I lift it as my father instructs and take Westlyn's hand in mine. "Don't watch. Close your eyes."

"I think it'll be worse if I don't watch."

"Are you sure?"

She nods. "Yes," she whispers. My lass is so strong. So brave.

I drag the blade across the center of her palm as lightly as I can to bring blood. I pierce my own and lace our fingers together so we're palm to palm. Blood, mostly mine, runs the length of our forearms, saturating our sleeves.

"Your wife is also your novice to teach and guide in the ways of our brotherhood. Do you accept responsibility for her?"

"Aye." I squeeze her hand, my eyes locked on hers. "I do."

"Repeat after me, Westlyn." My father states The Order decree, which they adopted from The Syndicate. It's something I've heard my entire life. "Do you swear to keep these vows?"

"I do."

I bring her hand to my mouth. "Your blood is my blood, as mine is now yours. From this day forward, we are one."

Westlyn is my wife. We've shared blood, and she's been incepted into The Order. She carries a piece of me inside her... our firstborn. One of many to come. It all gives me a fierce satisfaction. It isn't possible for her to belong to me more than she does now, yet I want to possess more of her.

Hold her. Stroke her silky skin. Feel her shudder with pleasure while my cock slides in and out of her.

I will do every one of those things later tonight when we're at home.

WESTLYN IS WEARING an ivory satin and lace gown fitting for a virgin on her wedding night. But my wife is no virgin, and she sure doesn't expect or want to be treated like one. The pregnancy hormones have made her insatiable the last few weeks.

One look at her in that satin and my cock is hard, throbbing with the need to be inside her. The closer she comes to where I'm sitting on the edge of the bed, the more I ache in my balls. "I've never seen you look more beautiful than today."

"And I've never seen you look sexier." My bride parts my legs and stands between them. She pushes my kilt up my thighs, her fingertips skimming through the bristly hairs on my legs. "The kilt is a nice change from the suit. Thank you for leaving it on."

"Anything to make my wife happy."

I pull up her gown and slowly slide my hand up the inside of her leg, feeling her thigh muscles quiver with tension. My fingers brush against her pussy, parting the soft lips, and I push the tip of my middle finger into her tight opening, using my thumb to massage her clit at the same time.

She bites her bottom lip and moans. "Mmm…"

"You like that, don't you, doll?"

She lifts one knee and rests it on the bed, giving me full access between her parted legs. "Mmm… hmm. Everything down there is so super sensitive lately. Feels so much more intense."

My finger smoothly glides in and out of her warm, slick hole. She rocks her hips against my finger, and a choked cry comes from her throat. "More?"

"Yes."

I insert another finger and fuck her with the pair, my thumb still rubbing her clit in a circular motion. My thrusts become harder, and she grips my thighs for balance. Reminds me of that first night together in the back of the limo when she was on her knees and had to use my legs to balance herself during the car ride.

Her head falls back, her eyes close, and her mouth parts. The pattern of her breathing instantly changes from calm and quiet to fast and labored. "Ohh… Kieran."

Fuck, I love hearing my name on her lips, but I especially love when it comes out as part of a breathless moan.

Her entire body tenses, and her fingers dig into the flesh on my thighs, painfully so. She cries out my name as her inner walls squeeze my fingers in release, the gripping motion making my dick throb to be inside her.

I revel in watching her come apart in my arms. I love that I'm able to do this to her. And I love that I'm the only man who's ever brought her to this kind of pleasure.

I grip the satin fabric and pull upward, tossing her gown to the floor. We're both bare, with the exception of my kilt. But it's staying on per my wife's request.

I slide my hands under her bum and pick her up as I rise to my feet, simultaneously flipping and lowering our bodies to the bed so that I'm topping her. But I ignore my aching cock and what he wants. This is our wedding night. I want this to be a night she never forgets; therefore, I am not finished bringing her pleasure.

I move down and begin with small kisses on the insides of her thighs, moving up until I reach my goal: her wet pussy—pink, swollen, and glistening from the orgasm I just gave her. "What are you doing?"

I always make sure she comes first, unless she wants to blow me, but then I move on to pleasing myself. I never give her two orgasms ahead of my own. "I'm going to make you come again."

"I don't think I can do it back-to-back like that."

"How do you know? I've never tried." I spread her folds apart with my fingers. "Relax. Let me do what I do best."

She spreads her legs farther apart and rocks her hips when I flick my tongue over her clit. Her hand moves to the top of my head, and she laces her fingers into my hair, lightly scratching my scalp with her freshly manicured nails. "You are so good at this."

I stop and swallow. "I know."

I push my tongue inside, tongue fucking her as deeply as I can, and tasting her recent orgasm. I savor every drop. I delight in every gasp and moan that comes from her lips as my tongue massages the bundle of sexual nerves in the roof of her pussy—that ultra-sensitive spot that evokes her strongest orgasms.

"Ohh... Kieran. I'm going to come again."

I knew I could fucking do it, but I didn't know I could do it that fast.

She trembles, her thighs quivering with ecstasy, and my mouth is flooded with her sweet juice. "Oh, fuck, Kieran..." She bucks her hips from the bed and grinds her pussy against my tongue.

I crawl up her body after she goes limp and releases my hair. I stop briefly to press kisses to her belly and then continue up her body until we're face-to-face. Heart-to-heart. Her arms wrap around my shoulders, and I feel her breasts pushing against my chest, her nipples like hard little pebbles.

I press a kiss to her mouth. "Mo chroí."

She smiles. "Mo chroí."

Her sweet smile. Her precious words. Both make my cock throb harder, begging for his release. My self-control tank is drained.

Fuck, I have to have her. Now.

I use my knees to push her legs apart and press the head of my cock against her drenched center, slowly sliding into her until I'm balls deep. "Ohh... fuck..."

Her wet flesh welcomes my cock and accommodates it. No matter how many times I take her, I'm always amazed by how tight she is. The way her body squeezes mine makes my spine tingle and my balls draw up against my body.

I slide my left hand into her hair to cradle the back of her skull, and I thrust into her over and over until I'm covered in a thin shroud of sweat. Her legs come up to hug my hips, and the different angle brings me into her even deeper. My wife's pussy is pure heaven.

I thrust one last time and drive my cock as deep as her body will allow. I lower my body to hers and kiss her mouth hard. "I fucking love you so much, Westlyn Hendry."

"I love you too."

I sink on top of her, supporting my weight with my arms on each side of her head. I stay that way, pressing sweet kisses against her lips, until my cock softens and slides out.

Westlyn and I coming together never fails to make me feel like we're fusing as one. Melding into one another. Losing ourselves in each other. Our bodies fit together perfectly as though each of us is one half of the other, and we can only be whole when together.

She is my other half. My better half. And that is why I will never let her go.

I was her kidnapper. I may have taken her as my captive, but she's the one who captured my heart.

EPILOGUE

KIERAN HENDRY

I'M on one side of the bed and Westlyn is on the opposite. Together we pull up the covers, and our two wee ones tuck the linens beneath their arms.

"Da, will you read with me?" Lachlan, our oldest, asks.

Our son loves books and stories. So thirsty for knowledge. Such a bright lad thanks to Westlyn's teaching and mothering. At five, he's already able to read on the level of an eight-year-old.

"No, I want to hear our story again. The one with princes and princesses and how we came to be." Our daughter, Bristol, never tires of hearing our family's story.

"What do you say, Lach?" I give him a wink, our secret sign that we'll pick up with last night's story after his sister is asleep.

He tries to wink back, but it comes off more like a squint. "Okay. I guess we can hear our story... *again*."

"Once upon a time there was a prince from a faraway kingdom who inherited the crown of a new kingdom."

"And the prince needed a princess." Barely four and my wee lass is already a romantic.

"Yes, baby. The prince needed a princess, but no ordinary princess. She had to be chosen from the royal family of his new kingdom's enemy."

"And the prince's enemy wouldn't give him his princess, so he had to ride in on his horse and kidnap her," Bristol says.

"That's right. He had three princesses to choose from and which one did he steal?"

"The bonniest one."

I look at Westlyn across the bed, her fingers laced and her hands resting on top of her swollen belly. "Aye, she was the bonniest one indeed. And still is."

"But the princess didn't like the prince because he was mean to her." Bristol punches my leg. "Bad Da for being mean to Mummy." She always scolds me when we get to this part of the story.

"The prince was mean to the princess, but he became sorry and full of regret for being cruel to her."

Bristol looks up at Westlyn. "Because the prince fell in love with Mummy."

I pet the top of my daughter's head when I see her eyes growing heavy. It always helps her fall asleep. "The prince did fall in love with the princess, and their marriage brought peace between the two kingdoms."

"And their princes and princesses were half of one kingdom and half of the other. Their children would forever bind the two lands, so they would never be enemies again." Westlyn's voice is soft and soothing.

Bristol yawns. "And they lived happily ever after."

I don't know why Bristol asks to hear this story. She's the one who ends up telling most of it.

My daughter closes her eyes, and Lachlan places his finger over his lips to shush me.

Westlyn leans down to kiss Lachlan. "I'm going to lie down while Da reads with you tonight."

She usually stays while he reads.

"Are you feeling all right?"

"Fine. Just aching in my back."

"Sure it's just a backache?"

She nods. "I'm fine. Stay and read with him."

Lachlan usually reads to us for thirty minutes every night, but I cut our time short tonight. I'm worried about Westlyn. With her last pregnancy, she complained of a backache, her water broke, and she delivered... all within three hours. We barely made it to Royal Infirmary before she got the urge to push Bristol out.

"Doll?"

"Just a minute, Kier," she calls out from the bathroom.

"Are you okay?"

"I'm fine." Her voice is calm, which eases my worry.

The door opens and Westlyn comes into the bedroom wearing one of her short, sexy gowns. "Pregnancy hormones doing crazy things again?"

She nods and walks toward the bed. "Very crazy."

She sits on the side of the bed and moves to the middle. "You know what I need, Mr. Hendry."

I start taking off my clothes, beginning with my tie. "I do know, Mrs. Hendry. Very well."

Westlyn is approaching her due date. Positioning has been tricky the last few weeks. "Tell me how you want it."

She rolls on to her side. "From behind."

"Not a problem, wife." I love rear entry.

"I didn't think you'd mind."

I lie on the bed and move behind her, kissing the back of her neck and shoulders. I do it to give her time to get wet, but I find that she's already drenching when I reach between her legs. "Always wet for me."

"Always."

I ease inside her, and it's impossible to suppress my groan. I pull back and thrust slowly, savoring the squeeze of her body around mine. "Fuck, I can't believe how tight you are."

How can she have given birth twice, almost three times, and still feel this virgin-tight? A woman's body can do amazing things.

I thrust a few more times. "Is this position good for you?"

She's tilting her bum upward, rocking to meet me with every stroke. "Mmm-hmm, but I want you to rub me. Make me come with you."

I reach around her pregnant belly to that sensitive place between her legs. She moans, and without a word, I know I've hit it. "Right there, Kieran."

I circle the whole area fast and hard. Slow and soft. Back and forth. Side to side. I give her a little of it all.

I move faster. My cock and fingers. "I want to feel your body squeeze me because you're coming so hard."

"Ohh... I'm coming, Kieran."

I bury my face in the back of her hair. "I love you, Westlyn. So fucking much."

She reaches over her shoulder and grabs the back of my head. "I love you, too."

I plunge into her one last time and hold that position while my balls squeeze until they're completely empty. When I finish, our arms, our legs, our entwined bodies collapse and go lax.

I pull out and reach for a pillow to place under her head. "Need one between your knees too?"

"Yes, please."

I spoon behind Westlyn, wrapping my arm around her waist and rubbing her tummy. This is baby number three, and the movement I feel beneath my hand still amazes me. "He or she is going crazy in there."

She places a hand on her belly next to mine. "I think this wee one will be coming soon."

Her due date isn't until next week. "Why do you say that?"

"I felt really good today." She always gets a burst of energy the day that she goes into labor.

"Then you should get some sleep, in case he decides to come tonight."

Westlyn's prediction comes to pass five hours later when her water breaks, and we rush to the hospital. Same as last time. She's barely admitted when she tells me that she needs to push.

We finally get to meet our next son or daughter.

Westlyn starts pushing, and the nurse tells her to stop because she needs to get the doctor.

"Hear that, doll? She's calling the doctor to come." I lean down and kiss Wes's forehead. "I love you so much."

She strokes my face with her hand. "I love you, too. But that doctor needs to come because I won't be able to stop pushing when I have another contraction."

"You have to breathe and not push."

"Yeah, right. Like that's going to happen. This baby is coming. It doesn't care who's ready."

Westlyn's physician comes into the room. "Oh... it's coming. I'm trying... but I can't stop it."

He hurriedly puts on a pair of gloves. No gown. "It's all right, Mrs. Hendry. Just means it's time to meet this wee one."

I watch the head of our third child emerge from my wife's body, and the doctor suctions his nose and mouth. Westlyn's legs are shaking, and she's breathing erratically when she reaches up to grab me. She pulls me down and squeezes me around the back of my neck. "It hurts, it hurts, it hurts."

"You're almost finished. Push him out."

Westlyn releases her ironfisted hold on me and works to catch her breath. She pulls her legs back, her eyes squeezed tightly, her brow wrinkled. A pair of tears escapes her eyes, and it breaks my heart to see her suffering in silence.

"Here he or she comes."

I hear a gush of fluid and then a piercing cry—our baby's first sound.

"It's a boy."

She falls against the bed, exhausted, and I kiss the top of her head. "You did it, Wes. We have another son.

He's placed on her chest where the nurses wipe him clean, cover his head with a blue beanie, and stuff him inside his mother's gown. Skin-to-skin.

Westlyn puts him to the breast, and it only takes a few minutes for him to figure out how to latch on. "Look at our boy, Kieran. He's so much like Lachlan and you."

"Ethan Graham Hendry." I lower my face so I can get a better look at my son. "I already love him as much as I do Lachlan and Bristol."

"Me too."

I look at our third child and know that I owe all of my happiness to Westlyn. Without her, I wouldn't know this kind of love and joy.

When I stole this beautiful woman, all I had in my heart was anger and rage and malice. I had cruel intentions. But then everything changed. My affection for her was unexpected. My love, unintended.

ABOUT THE AUTHOR

GEORGIA CATES

Georgia resides in rural Mississippi with her wonderful husband, Jeff, and their two beautiful daughters. She spent fourteen years as a labor and delivery nurse before she decided to pursue her dream of becoming an author and hasn't looked back yet.

Sign-up for Georgia's newsletter at www.georgiacates.com. Get the latest news, first look at teasers, and giveaways just for subscribers.

Stay connected with Georgia at:
Twitter, Facebook, Tumblr, Instagram,
Goodreads and Pinterest.

MEN OF LOVIBOND

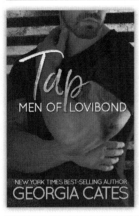 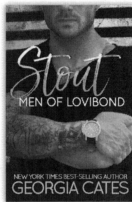 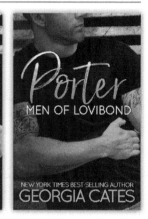

Sweet TORMENT

THE Beauty SERIES

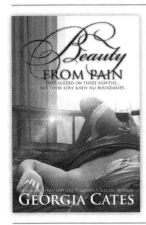

Dear Agony

A NOVEL

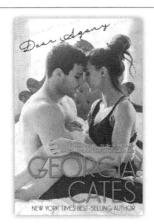

INDULGE

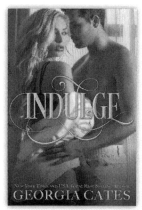

THE SIN TRILOGY

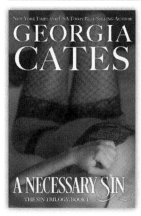 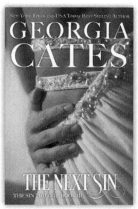 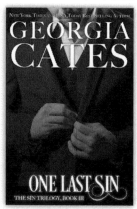

A SIN SERIES STANDALONE NOVEL

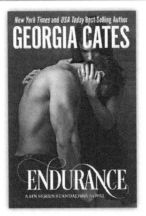

New York Times and USA Today Best-Selling Author

GEORGIA CATES

ENDURANCE

A SIN SERIES STANDALONE NOVEL

A SIN SERIES STANDALONE NOVEL

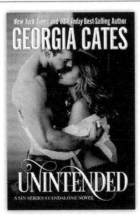

New York Times and USA Today Best-Selling Author

GEORGIA CATES

UNINTENDED

A SIN SERIES STANDALONE NOVEL

VAMPIRE AGAPE SERIES

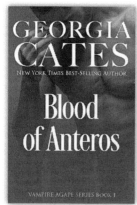
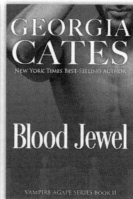
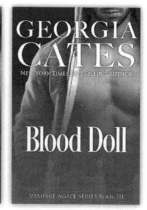

Made in the USA
Columbia, SC
03 November 2017